AMERICAN EPITAPH

James Laabs

First American Publishing

AMERICAN EPITAPH

By James Laabs

Published by:

First American Publishing
jameslaabs@yahoo.com

Copyright 2011 by James Laabs

ISBN 978-0-9767599-6-6 (print version)

PART ONE

Overthrow the effigy
The vast majority
Burning down the foreman of control
Silence is the enemy
Against your urgency
So rally up the demons of your soul

- Green Day, "Know Your Enemy,"
from the album 21st Century Breakdown

Entry One: April 2025

The sleek flying vehicle settled silently on the landing pad. The driver's side door slid open with a push of a button and Patrick emerged, wearing a silver jumpsuit. He bounded out of the car and stood for a few moments, enjoying the magnificent view of the modern city glistening in the sun. He walked to the rooftop entrance of his penthouse condo and pushed a button to open the sliding doors.

His apartment was sparkling clean, thanks to the robotic housekeeper who was on duty all day and night picking up after him. The housekeeper was one of several robots who made his personal life completely effortless.

He grabbed a cold beer and turned on the big screen TV that covered an entire wall of his spacious living room. The usual six channels came up, allowing Patrick to see the news, weather, sports and entertainment he most enjoyed. He settled into a heavily cushioned sofa and marveled how fortunate he was to be alive in the year 2025.

Patrick woke up, and had never felt more miserable. His head ached like someone had tapped at it with a hammer through the entire night and his throat was so dry he could barely swallow.

"Jeez, what a dream," he said to himself. His girlfriend Kristina was sleeping soundly beside him. She had enough sense the night before to avoid drinking the rum that their friend Jimmy brought to share with them. Jimmy had chastised Kristina for not drinking, reminding her that real bottled liquor was a rarity and hence needed to be enjoyed. It might be a year before he'd be able to get his hands on another bottle.

Kristina didn't drink, but she stayed up late into the night with them, listening to Jimmy's stories about what everyone thought the future was *supposed* to be like. When Jimmy was growing up in the 1960s, the notion of what the year 2025 would be like was the complete opposite of how it turned out in reality.

Patrick looked over at Kristina, who was snoring quietly, and wondered if she was having bizarre dreams like the ones he had.

Jimmy was an old-timer, born in the late 1950s, and reveled in giving Patrick and other young rebels history lessons on what the country had gone through in the past forty years. Jimmy usually started by reminiscing about the "era of prosperity."

He said, "It was a time when almost every able-bodied man and woman had a meaningful job that paid decent wages. The unemployment rate was five percent! Can you believe it? The country was filled with optimism. Those were the best years."

The era of prosperity was followed by what Jimmy called the "era of greed," a time when the economy grew so rapidly that everyone was chasing the brass ring of wealth. "The possibility that everyone could be wealthy seemed real at the time but it was all an illusion," Jimmy explained, "What everyone thought was the start of decades of prosperity was actually a house of cards. The government was spending money that it didn't have and running up outrageous debts. Then the people started doing the same thing, borrowing and spending money they didn't really have."

Jimmy's weathered face saddened as he talked about the "era of disillusionment," when expectations began to decrease to match the economic realities that were denied for so many years. Home ownership plummeted, savings accounts disappeared, incomes dwindled and unemployment skyrocketed.

"The government tried to cover up the facts with false statistics," Jimmy said, "but it eventually became apparent that the economy was hopelessly and permanently mired in shit. When the government said the unemployment rate was under ten percent but you knew a dozen people who were out of a job, it was pretty obvious they were covering up how serious things really were."

"The media called it *the new normal*," Jimmy practically spat the words out, "like coming up with a catchy name for it was supposed to make it acceptable."

Kristina and Patrick were both born in 1998, but by the time they were done with elementary school the country was already in the "era of decline."

Patrick didn't remember much about the good times, other than some snapshot memories of birthday parties and holiday celebrations where there seemed to be a mountain of gifts and an endless supply of food. Most of his memories were of the less pleasant times that followed.

"Enough daydreaming," Patrick said out loud. He rolled off the mattress that was lying on the floor and stood up. Getting water was the first priority – Jimmy said drinking lots of water was a good way to treat a hangover. Patrick grabbed a worn plastic pitcher and trudged outside to the well. The water was pretty clean in their area, usually clean enough that it didn't require boiling. They were lucky in that respect – in some areas the water was so full of poisons that it often couldn't be used even if it were boiled.

He filled the large pitcher to the very top and drank in large gulps as he walked back toward the house. By the time he was at the back door, half the pitcher was emptied.

Patrick tried to move silently around the house to avoid waking his housemates. He and Kristina shared the small home with two other couples, and everyone else was still sleeping. Even though they paid no rent – they were technically squatters – it took the contributions of three couples to keep the household running. Fortunately, the six of them got along very well with one another, and all contributed their time and ability to earn enough money to make sure they had enough food and the basic necessities.

The next task in Patrick's daily routine was to see if he could contact anyone else in the underground. Rebels in the area passed information primarily via shortwave radio and in person. The radio was an old vacuum tube model and a wire ran from the back of the radio through the ceiling to a small TV antenna on the roof. There was no television – at least for the lower class – but the unused dish worked as an antenna for the short wave.

"Good morning!" Patrick called hopefully into the microphone, "Is there anyone on the air this morning?" He paused for a few seconds, "Anyone on the air?" He paused again and waited. There was no response. Patrick was mildly disappointed, but finding other rebels on the shortwave was about a one-in-three chance. He would try again later.

Digital technology was alive and well in 2025, but the underground resistance preferred to communicate with one another using outdated analog devices. One reason was that the ruling class government had developed a nasty weapon called an e-bomb. When an e-bomb exploded, it released an ion storm that ruined all digital devices within a hundred yard radius, but did so without causing any damage to people or property. If the Freedom Troopers suspected a building was being used for rebel communications, they could lob an e-bomb through a window and render all the digital devices unusable.

A second reason for using analog communication was that the ruling class law enforcement frequently monitored digital signals from modern devices but had a very difficult time intercepting analog signals.

Regardless of whether it was digital or analog, all communication over the airwaves between rebels was done using a language that was part street slang and part secret code. So far, their communication code had not been cracked by the government.

Just then, Patrick felt two arms wrap around him from behind. "Good morning," Kristina said, "As much as I love you, I must say that you look like hell. And you smell like that awful liquor that Jimmy brought."

"I probably look worse than I feel. I'll be OK."

"Hopefully Jimmy made it back home last night," Kristina said.

"You don't need to worry about Jimmy; even at his age he can take care of himself."

"Any luck getting someone on the shortwave this morning?"

"Not yet, I'll try again in a while. I need to go out to the garden and get some work done before it gets too hot outside."

With the unemployment rate nearly fifty percent, most of the unemployed lower class was forced to become self-sufficient in order to survive. Many families had mini-farms in what used to be suburban back yards and some people manufactured small quantities of basic products in their homes, or provided services like mechanical repairs to their neighbors.

The house that Patrick and Kristina occupied had a three-acre yard that was lush, green grass at one time but now was used to grow vegetables and wheat. One of their housemates had assembled a crude machine in the garage powered by pedaling an old bicycle that allowed them to grind wheat into flour. The mini-farm and flour mill required an immense amount of work, but they earned enough from selling their crops and flour for the six people to scratch out a living.

After two hours of pulling weeds and hand tilling, Patrick took a water break in the shade. As he sat there, he saw Jimmy walking toward him through the neighboring backyards. He was sporting a Hawaiian-style shirt, khaki shorts, sunglasses, a wide brim straw hat and carried a long wooden walking stick.

It was highly unusual for Jimmy to be outdoors during midday. He hated the heat, for one thing. Jimmy was also a known opponent of the government and was sought for questioning on a regular basis. He found it was easier to avoid the Patriot Squads by traveling mostly at night and staying in the shadows. He typically didn't use the streets to travel, but walked through the fields and backyards as he was doing today.

"What brings you out in the sunshine?" Patrick asked.

Jimmy sat down on the bench next to Patrick. "Jesus, it's hot. It's that fucking global warming. But I come bearing a gift," he said as he pulled a shiny, eight-inch metal cylinder from beneath his loose fitting shirt.

"Is that what I think it is?" Patrick said excitedly.

"If you think it's a flash-bang grenade, then you're right," Jimmy said. "Someone found it and passed it on to me. I have big plans for how we're going to use this. That's what I'm here to talk to you about."

"Flash-bang" was a slang name for a concussion grenade. The nickname came from the blinding light and deafening noise the small bomb made. Anyone within fifty feet of a concussion grenade when it went off in an enclosed space was disabled and deafened for several minutes afterwards.

"What's your plan?"

"You know my thinking on strategy. When we get our hands on one weapon, it is imperative that we use it to acquire more weapons. Building a stockpile is the only way we can win. We use one little baby like this," Jimmy said, patting the flash-bang affectionately, "to steal twenty guns and grenades. If we use each of those twenty weapons to steal twenty more, that's twenty times twenty, or four hundred. If we do that a few times, soon we'll have thousands of weapons. That's when we can start to make some headway against those assholes."

Patrick nodded, but also thought that if what Jimmy were saying was true, the rebels would have had a huge arsenal built up already. Instead, all they had were small caches of weapons scattered in hiding places around the countryside.

Jimmy continued, "Here's the plan. The government gives those fucking nitwits in the Patriot Squads weapons and ammo to carry. They generally have twenty or twenty-five goons in every squad. My idea is to lure them into an enclosed space, hit them with the flash-bang, take all their weapons before they come to, and get the hell out before they know what hit them."

There were two types of military forces in 2025. The first was Freedom Troopers, who were full-time government soldiers. They were professional, well trained fighters who received good salaries and were armed with the latest weapons and equipment.

Because of limited funds, there were not nearly enough Freedom Troopers to provide a meaningful local police presence. That role was filled by Patriot Squads. Patriot

Squad soldiers were typically government sympathizers aspiring to wedge their way into the tiny middle class by making their loyalty known to the government. Patriot Squads were a step above pure volunteers and received part-time wages, similar to the Army Reserve of the early 2000s, although Patriot Squads were on active duty on a regular basis.

As far as the lower class majority was concerned, it was certainly prudent to have a healthy respect for government loyalists who were armed with deadly weapons, but the Patriot Squads were not greatly feared by the underground.

Jimmy continued describing his plan, "You know Joey Arcada, don't you?"

"Of course, he's a well-known asshole and leader of the Patriot Squads that patrol the Newtown area."

"Right," Jimmy said. "I've set it up so that he's going to find out about a big resistance meeting, supposedly being held tomorrow night at 10 p.m. at the old Veteran's Center. Joey Arcada wants desperately to be a Freedom Trooper. As an Area Leader, he's one step away from his goal. That makes him gullible. He's eager enough to take the bait without thinking twice that it might be a set-up."

"I've been in the Veteran's Center," Patrick said, "If we can get them all into the long hallway that leads to the meeting room, we can throw the grenade in there and put an entire squad out of commission long enough to take all their weapons."

"You catch on fast," Jimmy said approvingly, "but we need some way to get them all into the hallway."

"How about using a tape recorder set up in the meeting room?" Patrick suggested. "I've been rebuilding an old reel-to-reel and have some tapes and a microphone. We can record a bunch of people talking, and then play it real loud. We'll make sure the room is pitch dark so they won't figure out it's empty until it's too late. They'll all congregate in the hallway because it's the only way in and out of the meeting room."

"Can you get that tape recorder working by tomorrow?"

"No problem. Will it be you and me?"

"We'll need four people and some heavy-duty bags to put the weapons in after we take them. I have a perfect hiding place set up about ten miles from here, and a truck to transport the stuff. It's a great spot to stash the weapons, even the Freedom Troopers won't think to look there."

"You really think the Freedom Troopers will get involved looking for who did it?"

"Oh Christ, yes," Jimmy said, "If we pull this off, they'll bring Freedom Troopers in from other cities. The shit will hit the fan. They will search every suspected rebel location looking for those weapons. So we have to hide them in a place they would never suspect."

Entry Two: April 2025

Patrick recruited the two other men who lived in his house to help in the ambush. One of the things they had in common, and the main reason they lived together, was that they were all dedicated to the resistance.

When Kristina learned she was being left out of the attack, she burst into tears, ran to the bedroom, slammed the door and pouted. Patrick avoided her by staying in the garage and working diligently on the tape recorder, but a few hours later she finally approached him.

"Why did you ask Mike and Jason to be involved in the ambush and not me?" Kristina asked.

"I don't want you there; it could be dangerous. It could end up being hand-to-hand combat if the grenade doesn't knock everybody out. You're maybe five-six and a hundred pounds? How do you think you'd fare in close combat? Jimmy talks about these missions like they're some kind of grand adventures. But this whole thing could become four of us against thirty armed men if it goes wrong. I don't want you to get hurt, or worse."

"You're so full of shit," Kristina said angrily, "You know

how I feel. I'm ready and willing to do what it takes to help the resistance. I don't care about the risk involved."

"I'm sorry, baby, but I can't let you come along."

Kristina stormed out of the garage, slamming the door.

***

A small, rusty pick-up truck pulled in front of the house with the headlights off. Mike and Jason walked quickly to the vehicle and hopped into the open cargo bed. Patrick was just behind them, carrying a box containing the tape player, a battery and a speaker. He passed the box to Mike and hopped in the cab. Jimmy nodded to them and drove off.

After they hopped out and Jimmy hid the truck a block away, the men crept carefully into the dark building. Patrick used a small flashlight to survey the dark hallway and meeting room, and set up the tape player in a corner. The Veteran's Center meeting room and the hallway leading to it had cinder block walls, a concrete floor and ten foot ceilings – perfect for maximum effectiveness of a flash-bang.

Patrick connected the recorder and speaker to the battery and tested the set-up for a few seconds. It worked exactly as he had hoped; the sound was loud and realistic. Mike and Jason had helped him create murmuring and talking sounds and then Patrick overlaid their three voices over several tracks to create the effect of a realistic crowd. He made a loop to fill up the entire tape.

He checked his watch – there was still plenty of time. The four men sat on the concrete floor and talked quietly.

"Okay," Patrick said, "It's all set. The battery and tape will last sixty minutes, but that's it. So we shouldn't turn it on too early."

Jimmy threw a small walkie-talkie at Mike and said, "Go out front and hide behind those shrubs across the street. Keep a lookout in case they come early. Use the walkie-talkie to contact me when you see them arrive. Just push the red button and talk. I'm going to hide in the broom closet just off the hallway and listen. When I think all the goons are in the hallway, I'll roll the grenade out of the closet before they realize the meeting room is empty."

"What about us?" Patrick asked.

"I'll turn the recorder on about a half-hour early. You and Jason join Mike and hide outside the building. You'll hear the grenade explode from out there, don't worry. When you hear it, come in fast. But be careful in case there were any stragglers that didn't get knocked out by the grenade. We'll have about ten minutes to gather all the weapons and get them loaded in the truck."

Mike, Jason and Patrick knelt behind a thick hedge just outside the building. Patrick checked his watch again.

"There's no one around yet. Jimmy should be turning on the tape player in a little while."

Fifteen minutes later, a loud rumbling startled the trio. Two large trucks pulled up to the Veteran's Center front entrance and about thirty men poured out.

"Holy shit!" Patrick whispered, "There's the Patriot Squad...and even a couple of Freedom Troopers! We'd better let Jimmy know right now."

"Jimmy!" Mike whispered urgently into the walkie-talkie, "They just pulled up out front and they are heading in. There are about thirty of them."

"Okay, thanks," Jimmy answered.

"It looks like they really mean business," Jason said, "I hope Jimmy makes sure they're all in the hallway before he tosses the flash-bang. If any of those Freedom Troopers don't get knocked silly, he's a dead man."

They waited nervously for two minutes when they heard a loud *whoommp*. The three men sprinted through the front entrance and headed for the meeting room.

As they ran into the hallway, they saw that Jimmy had timed the grenade perfectly; almost every soldier was out cold on the floor, many of them sprawled on top on one another in the confined area. But still standing were two Patriot Squad soldiers who had trailed the others.

They were disoriented and blinded, but the two soldiers were still conscious enough to reach clumsily for their pistols.

Patrick threw himself at an unconscious soldier and grabbed the rifle from his hands. As he aimed at the two woozy Patriot goons, he hoped the safety was off and the action was set to automatic. The answer came quickly as a dozen armor-piercing rounds ripped open the chests of the Patriots. Within a split second, they had toppled backwards and lay on the floor in growing pools of blood.

Patrick got up slowly and walked over to the dead men. He removed their helmets. He recognized both of them; he had seen them at the market where he and Kristina sold vegetables and bread. The men had been there with their wives and children. Patrick's stomach began to churn and he turned away quickly.

There still was no sign of Jimmy. "Boss, are you all right?" Patrick shouted through the hazy darkness, being careful not to use Jimmy's real name. There was no answer. Patrick turned on his flashlight and started moving the beam around the room. Through the haze of smoke, he saw Jimmy standing in the doorway of the closet, the closet door itself hanging loosely on its hinges after the explosion.

"I can't hear a fucking thing!" Jimmy shouted, "I thought I would be safe in the closet with the door closed, but that grenade was more powerful than I thought!"

Patrick did a quick scan with his flashlight and checked the state of the rest of the soldiers. They ranged from totally unconscious to badly stunned. "Hurry up, let's get this done," he said to the others.

The four men had stripped all the soldiers of their weaponry and made two fast trips to the truck when a few soldiers started to show early signs of regaining consciousness. "We're pushing our luck," Jimmy said, "we don't want to be recognized. Let's get out of here."

With the cargo area piled full of guns, the four men crowded into the small truck cab. Their mood was jubilant.

"Man, did you see those two Patriot assholes? Their guts were ripped apart, right through their bullet-resistant jackets!" Mike said.

"I didn't want to kill those guys," Patrick said flatly, "but it was necessary. I only did it because I had to. I've seen them around town; they had wives and kids."

"I know you feel bad," Jason said, "but you had a split second to react to the situation. You did the right thing. It couldn't be helped."

They rode in silence for a few uncomfortable minutes.

"So where are we taking all this stuff, Jimmy?" Patrick asked.

"What?" Jimmy said loudly, still deaf from the explosion.

"Forget it," Patrick said, and the three young men laughed. Patrick had counted roughly thirty guns, lots of ammo, twenty bullet-resistant jackets, thirty grenades and some miscellaneous items. It was an enormously successful night. He made himself as comfortable as possible in the cramped truck cab and enjoyed the ride.

Entry Three: April 2025

With its cargo area filled with weapons and ammo, Jimmy drove the pick-up truck fast but carefully through the city and into the neighborhoods inhabited by the Wealthy class.

There were a few tense minutes as Jimmy passed a parked security vehicle. "Get down!" Jimmy said to the other three.

"We're packed in here like sardines! How can we duck out of sight?"

Jimmy relaxed when he saw that the Patriot soldier in the car was snoozing in the driver's seat with his head tilted back. "It's all right guys, he's taking a nap. I'll bet he won't be sleeping for long. Those guys we ambushed are probably waking up about now and reporting the attack."

The pick-up truck stopped in front of what was obviously the home of someone who was very wealthy.

"Are we going to rob this place and really finish off a successful night?" Mike asked.

Still partially deaf after being near the exploding concussion grenade, Jimmy didn't answer. He flashed the headlights on the truck three times. The large gate in front of the house opened slowly and Jimmy drove up a long, winding driveway toward the most impressive mansion Patrick had ever seen.

As they approached the house, one of the four garage doors opened and Jimmy pulled the pick-up inside. "Stay in here until the door closes completely," he ordered. Once the door closed, Jimmy got out and motioned the others to follow. Without a word, Jimmy grabbed an ammo box and started carrying it into the house.

"I guess we should grab some stuff out of the back and follow him," Patrick said to the others. They hurried to catch up with Jimmy, who had already disappeared through the door.

As Patrick entered, he saw a family of three standing in the kitchen. The man and woman appeared to be a couple in their fifties, and Patrick assumed the third person was a daughter who looked to be about twenty-five. They stood silently in a corner and watched the parade of deadly weapons pass by.

The men carefully deposited the weapons, ammo and bullet-resistant jackets in a large square opening that had been dug through the basement floor. Then Jimmy moved a heavy sheet of plywood over the five-by-five opening and covered the plywood with a large carpet.

"If someone's looking for it, they'll probably find it," Jimmy said, admiring the hiding spot. He appeared to have recovered from effects of the flash-bang. "But I can't imagine why anyone would think to search this place."

The men trudged up the stairs to the kitchen to find the family still there. Everyone stood uncomfortably for a few moments, when finally the husband spoke. "You'll forgive me if we don't make introductions," he said politely, "I trust Jimmy, but I think it's best if you other gentlemen don't know our names. I'm sure you understand why."

That was the most polite way anyone has ever told me they don't trust me as far as they can spit, Patrick thought. But he fully understood the reason for secrecy. This family was obviously ensconced in the Wealthy class, and it was just as obvious they were secretly supporting the rebellion. Their punishment would be fast and severe if they were caught helping rebels hide stolen weapons. Even with Jimmy vouching for his companions, the stakes were too high for the family to trust three guys who showed up in their kitchen in the dead of night.

Jimmy shook hands with the husband and headed for the door. Patrick and the other two men followed him and hopped into the now-empty cargo bed. Jimmy cautioned them to duck down and drove slowly down the driveway and out the gate, keeping the headlights off until they were blocks away from the mansion.

After they dropped the truck off, they walked the mile-and-a-half to Patrick's with everyone still in a celebratory mood.

"Jimmy, come on in. I think we have a batch of wheat beer that's ready to drink. Stay here tonight, it's too late for you to be out on the streets alone."

It took less than a second for Jimmy to agree. He looked tired and drained after the physical and emotional stress of the night. Patrick reminded himself that Jimmy was forty years older than the rest of them, although it was easy to forget because he acted much younger.

Kristina and the other women threw their arms around the men as they entered the house. "I'm so glad you're all right," Kristina whispered to Patrick. She released Patrick from her arms and turned to the others. "Let's sit down. I'm sure you've all had an exciting night and we want to hear all about it."

The telling of the tale took an hour and three bottles of beer apiece. All four men told bits of the story, and everyone laughed as Patrick joked about Jimmy's deafness after his close encounter with the flash-bang. Patrick omitted the part about killing the Patriot soldiers. He would tell Kristina about it later, but that part of the story didn't seem to fit with the celebration they were having.

None of the men revealed specifics about the hiding spot, and the women didn't ask. If any of them should ever be arrested and tortured by the Freedom Troopers, they were better off not knowing the details.

Mike's girlfriend Maria changed the subject by asking Jimmy to continue the history discussion they started a few nights earlier. "When all of the problems started in the country, I was really young. Exactly how did things become the way they are now? What happened?"

Jimmy took a long drink from his beer and gathered his thoughts. "The turning point was the election of 2012," Jimmy started, "but the problems started about four years before that. The world economy began to collapse in 2008, starting with the United States. At first it looked like it was just a very nasty recession and everyone waited for the economy to bounce back. After all, it always had in the past. But things didn't get better. A couple of years later, countries in Europe started going bankrupt and the European Union fell apart. Other parts of the world depended on the U.S. and Europe to buy all the crap they were manufacturing, so with the U.S. and European economies in the toilet, those other countries began to fall like dominoes."

"I remember reading about that," Kristina said, "the governments around the world tried to do all kinds of things to help but nothing worked to improve the economy."

"That's right," Jimmy said. "The world economy went from bad to complete shit within just a few years. There was simply too much to overcome – the governments around the world had screwed things up to the point that there was no way out. People were understandably angry and afraid. There were demonstrations and riots all over, but of course they didn't do any good."

"What happened in 2012?" Patrick asked. He had heard this story many times before, but Jimmy told it in such a compelling way that Patrick never tired of hearing it.

"People were bitter and grasping at straws for a solution. History tells us that when a situation like that exists, it opens the door for evil to seize power. And that's exactly what happened in 2012. The fascists started getting voted into office already in 2010. In 2012, their candidate was nominated by one of the major parties and won the Presidential election. Their candidate campaigned by promising to slash government spending and keep taxes low. But lurking behind their economic promises was a very sinister social agenda."

Kristina said, "I can't believe people would be that blind, to allow that to happen."

Jimmy was on a roll and continued, "They were very clever, those extremists. They appealed to people on an emotional level and of course they lied like crazy. Once they took power, they started implementing their social programs. They blamed the problems in the country on gay people, poor people on welfare, women who had abortions, the unions – they vilified everyone except themselves. And people fell for it."

Patrick added, "I remember in school, reading about a guy named P.T. Barnum who said, 'you can fool some of the people all of the time.' The thing that amazes me is they were able to convince working people that the Wealthy class should pay little or no taxes. Everyone was sold a bill of goods on the idea that if we let the rich keep all their money, their wealth would trickle down to the rest of the people."

"What a fucking joke that was," Jimmy said, "there were people making minimum wage paying twenty percent in taxes and people making fifty million a year who paid nothing at all. And of course the rich didn't let their wealth trickle down to anyone else. They kept all of it."

Patrick jumped in, because he had heard this part of the story many times, "The extremists that seized power supposedly were going to help the middle class, but in reality they themselves were controlled by the very wealthiest people, the top one percent. The wealthy already made a bundle in 2008 when the housing market collapsed. Many economists said that single event was the biggest transfer of wealth from the middle class to the upper class in the history of the world. By 2020, the middle class virtually disappeared – they lost their homes, their savings and their jobs. The rich got even richer and the middle class lost everything."

Mike had been dozing but woke up long enough to say, "Holy cow, that sucks."

"Now the wealthy finally had what they wanted," Jimmy said. "They had all the power. And they used it. But the economy was still so bad that most people went along with the craziness, at least at first. They were still hopeful that the extremists would fix the economy. People saw certain groups having their rights taken away and figured as long as it wasn't them, they went along. Since they weren't gay or collecting welfare or in need an abortion, they thought they were safe. They figured the persecution would stop there. But then the government started taking nearly everyone's rights away."

Kristina said, "I know this part all too well because I lived through it. My father was Caucasian and my mother was Hispanic. They couldn't understand it when the government outlawed biracial marriages. And I was pretty much forced to quit school because I was harassed non-stop by the administrators for being biracial."

"That was one thing they did," Jimmy said, "they also persecuted people who didn't practice the government-preferred religion, they drove anyone with a speck of brains out of the universities, deported millions of immigrants and reversed every civil rights law that had ever been passed. They also did away with the little bit of gun control that existed, with their ridiculous 'open carry' laws that turned cities into the Wild West for a while."

"But the politicians themselves got screwed in the end," Patrick said, trying to move the story forward.

"They got what they deserved," Jimmy said. "They were unwitting puppets all along, political hacks being used by the ultra-rich. Once they were elected, a few of them tried to do the right thing and quickly learned who was really in charge. Since the elections of 2020, which were completely fixed, there hasn't even been the appearance of a democratic government. The country is being run by a Board of Directors representing the top corporations in the world."

"And the majority of the population is just trying to survive," Patrick said.

"The country is divided into three classes," Jimmy lectured, "Of course there is the Wealthy class. They're maybe three percent of the population. Then there is the Employed class, which is not quite half the people."

"Yeah," Patrick said, "those are the people who work for the big corporations. All the manufacturing jobs are on the other side of the world, so most of the Employed perform menial service jobs for low wages. The corporations have figured out how to pay them just enough to get by and not cause a revolt. The Employed pay outrageous taxes – basically they give half their wages back to their employer, since the corporations and government are one and the same."

"That leaves the other fifty percent of the population," Kristina said, "the rest of us. They hold us in such low regard they don't even bother to give us a name. Mostly they just call us 'them.' People like us were forced to become self-sufficient in order to survive. And we *have* survived. We're getting by."

"We can't afford to rent a home, and certainly can't buy one," Patrick said, "but fortunately there are hundreds of thousands of foreclosed and abandoned houses so that the people who need a roof over their heads can just choose a place to squat. There are so many abandoned houses and so many squatters that no one bothers us. We're lucky to have a nice spot like this where we can have a little farm and earn a living."

"For now that's true," Jimmy said. "What if they decide to seize all the property and kick all the squatters out? As bad as conditions are now, things can always get worse."

Patrick said, "The government has their hands full right now. They're spending almost every dollar they take in trying to keep military order in the six countries that we occupy in the Middle East, Africa and Asia. And the resistance is chipping away from the inside."

"You're right," Jimmy said, "we're like ants at their picnic right now, a little bothersome but not too much trouble. We have to increase the pressure on them. The longer they stay in power, the harder it will be to get them out. I'm going to turn in now. It's been a helluva day. But tomorrow morning, we need to get back to business. We need to figure out how to make the most of those weapons we got tonight."

Entry Four: April 2025

As usual, Patrick was up early the next morning. Jimmy was already awake and munching on a slice of home-made bread.

"This isn't bad stuff," he said, pointing to the bread. "How late do you bums sleep in? The day's getting away from us. Can you roust everybody from their beauty sleep? We need to talk before I leave and I want to get home before the Patriot Squads start their morning rounds."

Within fifteen minutes, Jimmy was surrounded by a rather groggy and sullen group of pajama-clad rebels.

"That was a great job by everybody last night. It was a major victory for us. But we need to remember the need for secrecy. We not only made the government forces look like idiots, with two Patriot goons dead they'll be looking for revenge against whoever did it."

"What?" Maria said, "You didn't tell us that last night. What happened?" She elbowed Mike sharply in the ribs, "And why didn't *you* tell me about it?"

"It was self-defense," Mike said, "a couple of them didn't

get knocked out by the grenade and drew guns on us. Fortunately, Patrick reacted quickly and killed them before they killed us."

Kristina sat quietly. Patrick had told her the story as they lay in bed the night before.

Jimmy continued, "I shouldn't have to remind you to tell absolutely no one about what we did. And put your heads together to come up with a story in case you get questioned. Make damn sure your stories match up with each other because they'll be looking for inconsistencies."

"Is there a chance that any soldiers recognized you guys?" Kristina asked.

"I seriously doubt it," Mike answered, "Other than the two men Patrick shot, they were all semi-conscious at best. Plus it was practically pitch black in there and the grenade made a lot of smoke. We were careful not to use names or even talk much while we were hauling the guns out of there."

"Mike is right; I don't think we were recognized. We were all wearing black and had our collars up and hats on," Jimmy said. "Be ready to be questioned just in case, that's all I'm saying."

"Any ideas on what we're doing next?" Patrick asked.

Jimmy answered, "I think we're going to sit tight for a

couple of weeks and let this blow over. We definitely shouldn't react to any intelligence that we hear; my guess is that they will try to return the favor and feed us some false information to get us out in the open. What I'd like to do over the next few weeks is to recruit and organize."

"I love that idea, Jimmy," Kristina said, "even if we tell no one about last night, the word will leak out. I think it will give people in our sector hope that the resistance can win. That will help us get more people to join."

"Let's not limit our thinking to just one sector," Jimmy said, "I think it's time to expand." He pulled out a crude map. "Patrick, you and Kristina travel each week to the marketplace in the sector north of here. Chat with people who are buying your produce, see if they've heard about what happened. If they seem like they're on our side, talk to them. But be careful; don't say too much at first."

"Mike and I will go west," Maria volunteered, "We both have family there and I'm sure they would join us. They surely know others that will be interested."

"Same for Megan and me," Jason said. "My aunt and uncle live in the sector to the south of here, and I know they're supporters of the cause."

"Now we're making progress," Jimmy said, "but be very careful about what you say and to whom. I've got to get going. Remember what we talked about – watch what you say, and be prepared for some heat about what happened last night. Let's get together again two weeks from today." And with that, Jimmy thanked everyone for their hospitality and walked out the door.

Entry Five: April 2025

A loud engine noise disturbed Patrick's idle thoughts as he worked in the backyard farm. He walked around to the front of the house to investigate and saw an open-backed troop carrier with two Freedom Troopers in the cab and a dozen Patriot Squad soldiers sitting on benches in back. The camouflaged truck drove slowly past the house and stopped about fifty yards down the road.

The Patriot Squad soldiers piled out and gathered around the two Troopers, who began pointing to various houses on the street and barking orders. The soldiers broke into groups of three and dispersed from the truck. Patrick walked quickly into the house.

"There's a Patriot Squad here in the neighborhood. Are we all set with our stories?" he asked everyone.

Kristina answered, "It's not that hard for us; our story is that the women were here all night at the house. You guys went out for a couple of hours."

"And where did we go, guys?" Patrick asked.

"We went hunting in the dark for rabbits with flashlights and slingshots," Mike said, "didn't have any luck, though. We gave up after a couple of hours and came home empty handed. You missed a couple of easy shots, Patrick, so we ate vegetable stew. Way to go."

"Let's be serious, all right?" Patrick said. "And don't overdo it. The fewer details the better."

Twenty minutes later, there was a loud knock on their door. Patrick opened it to find three Patriot Squad soldiers, looking stern and solemn.

The soldier nearest the door said brusquely, "We're investigating some trouble that occurred last night. We need to search your house and talk about the whereabouts of everyone who lives here." He motioned to his companions, who followed him as he forced himself uninvited into the house.

They did a thorough search of the house, the garage, and even walked around in the farm field. When the soldiers completed the search, they came back into the house and the lead soldier asked, "How many residents are there living here?"

"Six of us, three men and three women," Patrick answered.

"All right, you two stay here with me," the lead soldier said to Patrick and Kristina, then motioned at the other four and said, "take them into separate rooms and question them."

The questioning was what Patrick expected for the first ten minutes, the Patriot goon asking where he and Kristina were the night before and whether they saw anything out of the ordinary in the neighborhood. But Patrick noticed the longer the questioning went on, the more and more agitated the soldier became. "You two are known as troublemakers. I've seen you around Newtown, especially you," the soldier said, looking at Kristina, "shooting off your mouth about how badly the government treats you and your kind. By rights, I can make one of you move out of this shithole, and cite you for interracial cohabitation."

"Who said we're together?" Kristina said angrily. "We're just living in the same house to make ends meet. I can't afford to live in a house alone; I'm not a toady of the government like you."

The soldier raised his rifle butt as if he was going to hit Kristina in the face, but pulled back when Patrick stepped in front of her.

"I'd love to stay here and teach you a few things," he said to Patrick, "but we have too many people to question yet today. And frankly, I think you're both too stupid to pull off the crime we're investigating. But I'm going to keep an eye on this neighborhood." He turned to Kristina and leered, "I'll see you around town."

As they walked out of the house, one of the soldiers threw a flyer on the floor that read:

$25,000 REWARD
FOR INFORMATION LEADING TO
THE ARREST AND CONVICTION OF
THOSE RESPONSIBLE FOR THE
MURDER OF TWO MEMBERS
OF THE PATRIOT SQUAD

"That wasn't so bad," Mike said, once the soldiers were walking down the street.

Patrick frowned and said, "Our session didn't go so well. But they're grasping at straws, going door to door. The guy we talked to became frustrated and tried to intimidate us into talking. That's a sign they're just flailing around – they don't have a clue as to who did it."

Hopefully no one in the neighborhood will tell them they saw us get into a truck and ride away," Jason said.

"Jimmy was quiet and had the headlights off," Mike said. "It was dusk by the time Jimmy picked us up, so everyone was inside for the night."

In 2025, there was little electricity available to the masses and none for the lower class. The Wealthy and most of the members of the Employed class had electrical service, but most households relied on some sort of homemade device to generate electricity. Patrick's house had stationary bicycles connected to batteries – two people peddling an hour each day provided the house with enough electricity to power five light bulbs and a small electric water heater for a few hours. Other houses had windmills and some that were close to a river or creek used crude hydropower.

As a result of limited availability of electricity, most people's schedules tended to follow daylight hours. It was common for the parts of the city other than where the Wealthy lived and shopped to be completely empty by nightfall. Streetlights were a thing of the past in most areas and the chance of being robbed while walking the streets alone after dark was high.

"Let's remember what Jimmy said," Patrick reminded the group, "as tempting as it is to talk about our victory last night, it's critical that we keep quiet. You know what the consequences are if we're caught."

"You don't need to remind us," Jason said, "these days you get one trial, even for capital punishment cases. The legal system is much too overcrowded to be bothered with appeals."

"And judges don't hesitate to issue the death sentence," Mike added, "capital punishment is not only legal but it's encouraged by the government. If we were caught we'd be tried and judged by our so-called peers, every one which would be Wealthy or Employed, and we'd surely be in front of a firing squad within a month."

"We all recognize what's at stake, and we know we have to keep this between ourselves," Kristina said, putting an end to the grisly discussion.

Entry Six: April 2025

The six members of the household spent the remainder of the day harvesting vegetables, milling flour and baking bread for the markets the next day. Patrick and Kristina traveled each week to the People's Market, which was held every Saturday in Center City, about twenty miles north. There was a smaller market on Saturdays in their home city of Newtown, which Mike and Maria usually attended.

Saturday morning, Kristina and Patrick were up early to pack their produce in baskets and haul it to Center City. How they traveled to the market depended on how much they had to sell on that particular day. If they didn't have a large load of produce, they rode bicycles and pulled a small trainer behind them for the twenty mile trip. On this day, the load of bread, flour and vegetables was substantial and all six household members pitched in to haul it to a meeting point where a truck picked up sellers who were traveling to the People's Market. In exchange for one-tenth of their day's sales, Kristina and Patrick shared the back of the semitrailer with several other vendors who were selling their wares in Center City.

The talk among those traveling to Center City was the death of the two Patriot Squad members.

One woman said, "I sure wish I knew who it was who killed those soldiers. I'd turn them in without a second thought. I could do a lot with that $25,000."

A man nearby answered, "You would turn in your own neighbors? How many people do you know who've been beaten up or murdered by those Patriot goons? If I knew who it was that killed two of them I'd shake their hands and thank them."

Kristina and Patrick sat quietly, not wanting to get involved in the discussion. A third passenger in the truck said, "Was it rebels or criminals? If it was a gang that did it, maybe you'll be looking down the barrel of one of those stolen guns someday soon."

"A gang wouldn't be that organized," another man said, "I heard some Patriot Squad guys talking and they said it was a commando group of some kind; they were really professional, well-armed and knew what they were doing."

Patrick had to hide a smile. Jimmy was pretty calm before and during the ambush, but the other three men struggled to control their bowels. Of course, the Patriot goons who were there that night would exaggerate the professionalism of their attackers; they would never admit to being overcome by three farmers led by an old man.

About ten miles south of Center City, the truck passed a brick building on the right side of the road. Patrick often wondered what it was, because it had the bleak, utilitarian appearance of a government military facility. Patrick opened the window leading to the cab and shouted to the driver, "Hey, do you know what that building is?"

"Yeah," the driver yelled back, "and it's none of your business. Keep quiet and enjoy the ride."

After they arrived, Patrick approached the driver. They had some friendly conversations in the past, and he couldn't understand why the driver was so short with him.

"Hey, Charlie," Patrick said, "what's up? I didn't mean to upset you by asking about that building; I was just curious is all."

The driver led Patrick well away from the group of sellers who were unloading their wares and whispered, "It's an armory; where they store weapons and hold training for all the military in an eight-sector area. There are enough guns in that place to arm hundreds of men, maybe a thousand. I know this because I have a close friend who works there as a janitor. He and I share the same viewpoint on certain matters, if you know what I mean." Charlie looked at the ground and shuffled his feet nervously.

Patrick met Charlie's eyes with his. "There are more and

more people who have the same viewpoint. Maybe we can get together sometime and have a beer."

"That would be good," Charlie said, "let's plan on doing that soon. The sooner the better."

The People's Market was busy on a sunny, warm day. During times they weren't talking to customers, Patrick told Kristina about his conversation with the truck driver.

"Do you think you can trust him?" she asked.

"Yeah, I do. He's definitely genuine. We were both dancing around the subject, being careful. Obviously, I won't say anymore to him until I talk to Jimmy. That armory could be our next attack. If we got our hands on all of those guns the rebels would become a force to be reckoned with overnight."

Kristina said, "Didn't Jimmy say we needed to be careful about the government feeding us false information? What if this is a trap?"

"It's highly unlikely it's a trap," Patrick answered, "but I wouldn't ever think of doing anything without Jimmy's go-ahead anyway. So I'll tell Jimmy and let him decide how to handle it."

"What about moving all those weapons? Even if you were able to get into the armory, where would you keep all the guns you took? There's a lot to think about that you haven't considered," Kristina said.

Patrick sighed and answered patiently, "You're right. And we'll need a lot of men. I'll bet that place is heavily guarded. I know it's a long shot that we'll be able to make this happen, but it's still worth looking into."

Kristina changed the subject by saying, "The conversation in the back of the truck on the ride here was interesting. People are divided, it seems like some people are anti-government, a fair number are pro-government and many don't care one way or the other."

"Jimmy talks a lot about apathy," Patrick said. "He says that was one of the main reasons why the country fell apart. It's hard to believe, but over half the people didn't bother to vote in many elections, even when things were falling apart and their vote meant so much. That's how the extremists got into power, because there were so few people voting."

"What I don't understand are people in the lower class being pro-government. Of course, the Wealthy have a strong interest in keeping the status quo. The Employed, most of them are too tired from eking out a living to care one way or the other, but I know quite a few of them are pro-government. What surprises me is that there are so many people in the same situation as us who are apathetic," Kristina said.

"I don't understand it either, but Jimmy says it's a carry-over from the past thirty years. Attitudes like that change very slowly. But not everyone is apathetic; there are plenty of people who support the rebellion."

"Many people keep their opinions to themselves because the odds are so stacked against the rebels. And if you're branded a rebel, you can end up in prison or worse," Kristina said.

"I agree with Jimmy that it's like a snowball. The success we had the other night will bring more people into the cause. And if we pull off something like the armory, it could really get things going for us."

Entry Seven: April 2025

Patrick and Kristina returned home from Center City in the early evening exhausted as usual but with enough cash in their pockets to keep the household operating for another week. Mike and Maria also had a successful day at the Newtown market, so the mood in the house was happy on that Saturday night.

The group of six sat that evening and discussed the events of the past few days. Mike said, "the Newtown Market was swarming with Freedom Troopers today. Some of them even had those horrible masks on and were carrying gas grenades."

"That's just an intimidation method," Maria said. "They're trying to frighten people. But I admit, seeing the Freedom Troopers in those masks is a frightening sight."

"Jimmy said that there would be more Freedom Troopers showing up around town," Kristina said, "there aren't enough of them to be a major presence everywhere, so the government shuffles them to cities where there's rebel activity. Newtown is apparently a hot spot right now."

"I can't help thinking this is my fault," Patrick said to the group, "I've thought over and over about what happened the other night. I reacted on instinct. If I would have thought for a second, I would have realized those two soldiers were barely conscious. I could have just clubbed them instead of shooting them."

"Don't beat yourself up over this," Megan said. "You shooting those soldiers probably saved all of your lives. Also, what if you had let those two guys live and they recognized you? Stop worrying; you did the right thing."

"I also brought a lot of heat down on the local rebels. That may not have happened if no one was hurt in the ambush," Patrick said.

"I disagree," Mike said, "Remember, we stole a bunch of guns! They would be plenty pissed off even if no one had gotten hurt. Look at the bright side of things; we now have a pretty good weapon stockpile."

"How did things go today in Center City? Did you get a chance to talk to anyone about the rebellion?" Jason asked.

Patrick told everyone the story of the truck driver and his knowledge about the armory. Both Jason and Mike were immediately excited.

"That's amazing!" Mike said. "Let's get in touch with Jimmy and let him know!"

"We better not move too fast," Patrick cautioned, "Jimmy said that we need to lay low for a couple of weeks and I think that's good advice. Like you said, Newtown is swarming with military right now. We should let things settle down."

"Did you meet anyone else in Center City that could help the resistance?" Megan asked.

Kristina answered, "I had a few good conversations with people. It was easy, since even in Center City everyone wanted to talk about the attack the other night. And of course every person seemed to have an opinion about it. I tried to get the people who seemed pro-rebellion into conversations. My sense is that we can attract a pretty big group of supporters in the Center City area."

"I think that's true here in Newtown too," Maria said, "I'd say about half the people I spoke with were pro-rebellion."

"There's a big difference between being a casual supporter of the cause and being willing to put your life on the line," Patrick said, "that's the challenge we have, to find people who are committed enough to take action."

Entry Eight: May 2025

The next two weeks passed uneventfully. Patriot Squads and Freedom Troopers were out in force and patrolled the areas in and around Newtown. But the government investigation of the ambush uncovered no suspects and within a few days, everyone in the household relaxed into their usual routines.

Visits into Newtown were unusually tense because the city was where the Freedom Troopers were concentrated. The crime rate plunged because criminals knew Troopers were on patrol constantly. The Freedom Troopers grew more frustrated each day that the murders were not solved, and they took their frustrations out on the lower class residents of the city. Patrick heard that harsh public beatings of petty criminals by Freedom Troopers were a frequent occurrence.

One night around nine, there was a knock at the back door of the house. Patrick looked out and saw Jimmy, accompanied by an extremely large, tough-looking man.

"Hi Patrick," Jimmy said casually. "Meet my friend Danny. He was a professional wrestler back early in the century; his wrestling name was 'Deadly Danny.' As of two weeks ago, he has started hanging out with me, in exchange for a small stipend. I like to move around at night, and for the past two weeks it's been a dicey proposition walking around alone. The Patriot Squads are less likely to hassle people in pairs, especially when one is as big as Danny."

"Good meeting you Danny," Patrick said. He didn't extend his hand. Danny didn't look like the hand shaking type.

"Yeah," Danny answered, "You got any beer? Jimmy said you would have some."

"Let's go sit down and I'll get you one," Patrick said. The other household members heard Jimmy's voice and appeared in the living room.

Patrick told Jimmy about the trip to the People's Market and his brief talk with Charlie the truck driver.

"We have to be absolutely sure this guy isn't a government spy," Jimmy said, "I want to meet him before this goes any further."

"That would be great, it's a good idea to be careful," Patrick answered, "but think about it, Jimmy. Kristina and I have been riding in Charlie's truck a couple times a month for three years now. We've had quite a few very friendly conversations over the years. Do you think he's been doing that for the past three years just so he can set us up now?"

"You never know, maybe the government just approached him this week and paid him off. The timing seems too good to be true. I want to meet him."

The talk turned to the logistics of attacking the armory. Jimmy said, "From what little I know about that place, it's loaded with security systems and guarded by a bunch of soldiers."

"How many guards do you think there are for the whole armory building?" Kristina asked Jimmy.

"I would bet there are quite a few. I've driven by that place on the way to Center City. Never knew what it was before, but I figured it was some sort of government building, since there are security cameras all over on the outside. It doesn't look that big, maybe five thousand square feet. Weapons don't take up that much room. You can fit a lot of guns in a pretty small space."

"What about moving the stuff? And where would we put it?" Mike asked.

"I have some ideas on that, Mike," Jimmy answered confidently, "it's getting in and out of there without getting ourselves killed that worries me the most."

"You and everybody else," Kristina said. "Are you sure we're ready for this big of an undertaking?"

"It's time to start making some big moves. But we need to

find out lots more about it," Jimmy said. "Patrick, see if you can talk to that truck driver and set up a meeting for you and me, this Charlie guy, and his janitor friend."

"Sounds like a plan," Patrick said.

Jimmy clapped a dozing Danny on the shoulder. "Wake up my friend, it's time to go." They walked out the back door and disappeared into the darkness.

Entry Nine: May 2025

Early one morning, Patrick watched out the front window as a semi-truck cab stopped in front of the house. It was Charlie the truck driver and his friend, Stan, who worked as a janitor at the armory. "They're here!" Patrick called out.

Jimmy had come over late the night before and stayed overnight, so Charlie and his friend were greeted by seven people packed into the living room.

"Quite a crowd here," Charlie said suspiciously.

"We can all be trusted," Jimmy answered quickly, "the question is, can we trust you?"

"I've known Patrick for a few years now," Charlie said, "and I consider him a friend. Stan and I have been waiting for some kind of credible resistance to organize before we stuck our necks out, and you seem to have done it. I'm assuming that you folks were the ones who ambushed the Patriot Squad a few weeks ago."

"Whether that was us or not doesn't matter," Jimmy said, "the point is that we can get our hands on enough weapons to arm twenty rebels. Is that enough for us to take the armory?"

Stan spoke up, "Twenty would definitely do it; in fact I think fifteen would be enough. If the armory were attacked in the middle of the night, there would be twelve Patriots and one Freedom Trooper on duty. Most of those clowns fall asleep on the night shift even though they're supposed to stay awake. If it were done right, you could overcome them before they know what hit them."

"Tell us everything you know about the building," Jimmy said.

Stan sketched a map of the building on a piece of paper as he talked, "There's an outer hallway that rings most of the building except the delivery and loading dock. There are four entrances including the loading area. Actually there are five entrances – one is an emergency exit and that's how we'll get in. The idiot guards have disabled the alarm on it and adjusted the cameras and motion detectors so there's a big blind spot outside that door. That way they can sneak out there and smoke without setting off an alarm or being on camera."

"Inside, it's a big open room with a twenty-five foot ceiling. There's a metal gangway about fifteen feet up that's on three sides of the big room. The guards are posted in these locations," Stan said as he marked his map.

"Everything is stored in the open central area: guns, bullet-proof jackets, grenades of all kinds, a few rocket launchers and some e-bombs. The thing we have to be careful of is security. There are cameras and motion detectors throughout the building and the perimeter outside."

"Can you do anything about the security system?" Jimmy asked.

"I can cut the wires on the motion detectors," Stan explained. "It'll take about a minute for an alarm to indicate that the security system isn't working. I can do the same with the cameras. There's one soldier that monitors the cameras and security system. He'll notice the screens go dark, but he'll wonder what happened for at least a minute. The guy is half asleep most of the time. One minute should be more than enough time for you to get from the entrance to anyplace in the building."

Stan added, "I don't want to seem cocky, but I know pretty well about how things work on the night shift. I've worked it for a long time. The Patriot soldiers are a lazy bunch of slack-asses. I suppose it's human nature – nothing out of the ordinary has ever happened to make them believe someone would dare to attack the armory. They're fat and complacent and bored. If you surprise them, I don't think they'll put up much of a fight."

Jimmy thought for a minute and then presented a detailed plan to the group. Stan agreed that it was brilliant.

"How will we coordinate when this happens?" Charlie asked.

"You're on the shortwave, right?" Patrick said, "let's plan on the time to be precisely 4 a.m. We'll set the date over the air. That means, Stan, that at 4 o'clock sharp you cut the wires on the security."

"I think we should do it one day next week," Jimmy suggested. "I need a few days to line up some volunteers. I'll let you know."

Entry Ten: May 2025

On his routine scan of the airwaves a week later, Patrick was surprised that his call was answered by Jimmy. Usually Jimmy's method of contact was to drop in out of the blue and knock on the back door of the house. Using their established system of code words, Jimmy let Patrick know that he would pick him up that evening, for as Jimmy put it, "an errand."

At about eight o'clock a well-worn, sub-compact car that had been converted to use natural gas pulled up in front of the house. Patrick was keeping an eye out and spotted Jimmy behind the wheel. He ran out quickly and hopped into the passenger seat.

"Nice wheels," Patrick said, "where'd you borrow it?"

"This isn't borrowed; it was donated to the cause."

"Nice. Can I ask who donated it?"

"We're heading to his house right now. Remember the place where we stashed the guns? That's who gave me the car. The rebellion in this area gained some respect a few weeks ago, Patrick. People are starting to take us seriously, including our wealthy friend we're going to visit. He's worried about me being out on the streets at night. He got one look at my bodyguard Danny and decided a car would be a better way for me to get around safely."

"What are we doing there? Exactly who is this guy?"

"His name is Mark Johnson. He's a big shot in a company that mines some rare mineral, and he's been advising me on how to build our organization. He suggested that I have a replacement trained and ready to take over in case something happens to me. That's where you come in, Patrick."

Patrick sat in shocked silence for a few seconds. He managed to mumble something about being honored Jimmy had chosen him.

"Don't start getting weepy on me. I plan to be around for a long time so let's not make this more than it is. However, I think Mark is right – we *are* in a dangerous business and having you ready to step in if necessary is an excellent idea."

Like their previous visit, Jimmy flashed his headlights, waited for the gate to open and drove straight into a vacant spot in the large garage. They saw Mark Johnson standing by the door into the kitchen.

Jimmy greeted Mark Johnson with a bear hug and received a weak hug in return from their host. "Mark, I'd like you to meet Patrick, the kid I've been telling you about."

"A real pleasure, Patrick," Mark said as they shook hands, "Jimmy speaks quite highly of you. Come in, both of you."

Jimmy outlined the plan to break into the armory, and the three men discussed strategy for a half-hour. As they wrapped up their strategy session, Mark said to Jimmy, "I'd like to talk to you privately for a few minutes. Patrick, will you excuse us?" The two got up and left Patrick sitting at the kitchen table.

Patrick saw the daughter walking down the hallway toward the kitchen. As she came through the doorway, it was obvious that Patrick's presence had startled her. "Oh! I thought Jimmy was the only one here. That's the way it usually works. My name is Jenna, Jenna Johnson."

"*Jenna Jenna*?" Patrick asked awkwardly.

Jenna giggled and said, "Of course not! It's Jenna Johnson."

Patrick suddenly became engrossed in examining the top of the kitchen table and felt his ears growing red. To any male in his late twenties, Jenna Johnson was the ideal of female perfection. Long blonde hair cascaded onto her shoulders, and her tank top and shorts showed off a tanned, toned body. She carried herself with an air of confidence and careless arrogance that only a Wealthy class girl could do.

Jenna mistook Patrick's shyness for aloofness. After a minute of uncomfortable silence she said, "I suppose you think I'm a stuck-up rich girl who has had everything handed to her."

"Uh, no...I don't think that at all," Patrick answered defensively.

"You may not believe this," Jenna said indignantly, "but the Wealthy don't have it as easy as you think. My parents have to put up this huge front every minute of every day. We have to go to church every week – the *right* church – even though my parents really aren't very religious. When I'm at the university, I can never step out of line or disagree with anything the professor says. If I do, it might reflect badly on my father."

Patrick tried to interrupt by saying, "I didn't..."

"No, of course you didn't know that," Jenna said angrily, "and if I did something that reflected badly on my father, he could get fired from his job. My dad always says that it's a short drop from the sidewalk to the gutter. We have to be careful of every word we say in public, every movement we make. So don't try to tell me that we have an easy life!"

Fortunately for Patrick, Jimmy and Mr. Johnson came walking back into the kitchen at that moment. "Oh, I see you two have met," Mr. Johnson said, "all right then, you gentlemen take care getting home. Jimmy, don't forget to stop at the nat-gas dispensing station outside the garage and charge your tank."

As they drove off, Jimmy said, "Sorry that we had to step away. Mark has a friend who will let us use a large private room in his warehouse to store the stuff we take from the armory. You've come a long way in Mark's eyes – he likes you – but he doesn't quite trust you all the way yet."

"That's understandable," Patrick said, "we're lucky that we have guys like Mr. Johnson supporting us. But I have to wonder why people like him do it. What's in it for them?"

"All Mark wants is for things to return to the way they were at the turn of the century. Some of those in the Wealthy class think everyone should have the same rights, regardless of their race, religion or sexual preference. There aren't many of them that hold those beliefs, but there are a few."

"So we're picking up the guns from Mark's basement tomorrow night?"

"Yup, I'll borrow that pick-up truck again. We'll take the guns right from there to load in Charlie's semi," Jimmy said, "The next morning we hit the armory. Get plenty of sleep tonight because we'll be up all night tomorrow."

Entry Eleven: May 2025

Jimmy had carefully recruited a squad of fourteen to raid the armory. Patrick, Jason and Mike were on the team, and surprisingly Kristina talked Jimmy into being part of the operation.

Patrick asked Jimmy, "Can we trust these guys you found?"

"I have complete faith in them," Jimmy answered, "These are people I've worked with on little things over the past year. They've all had experience in skirmishes with the Patriot Squads. Not as intense as what we're heading into, but I think they can handle it."

Everyone sat in the semitrailer about two hundred yards from the armory. Five minutes before the appointed hour, Jimmy motioned all the uniformed rebels to follow him on foot. They approached the building quietly and gathered just outside the emergency entrance, being careful to stay in the security system's blind spot that Stan had diagrammed.

At precisely 4 a.m. Jimmy said, "Let's *go*!"

The plan was simple. Four pairs of rebels moved swiftly to each of the guard posts at the entrances. The remaining seven rebels headed for the central core where the weapons were located.

The rebels dispatched the entrance guards with little resistance. As soon as the guards were taken care of, the eight rebels moved quickly and quietly toward the central core to support their comrades. By the time they made their way to the central core, a screeching alarm pierced the air.

Patrick and Kristina were part of the group led by Jimmy that went straight for the central storage area. Mike and Jason were among the teams that attacked the guards stationed at the entrances.

As Mike ran into the central core, he yelled, "We got the guards at the entrances! There should only be nine of them left!"

"I like the odds – let's finish them!" Patrick screamed at the top of his lungs as he shot at the Patriots who had awoken from their slumber and were stumbling haphazardly into the core area.

Following Jimmy's plan, the rebels had spread themselves strategically around the central core area and picked off the government soldiers one-by-one like ducks in a shooting gallery as they entered the core area. The ground floor now belonged completely to the rebels.

On the catwalk above, one remaining Patriot ducked for cover and the lone Freedom Trooper, with his ranks decimated, ran into the monitor room located in the upper level.

"We have to get them fast!" Jimmy said. "We can't let them call for help."

The Freedom Trooper did pick up a phone to call for help, but Stan had disabled the outgoing communication lines and the thick metal and stone walls prohibited wireless communication. When calling for help failed, the Trooper reluctantly opened what the guards called the "Armageddon Cabinet." He never imagined that he would need to use the weapon that the cabinet held.

As the rebels searched for a way up the stairs to the catwalk, the Freedom Trooper appeared, holding what looked like a gigantic rocket launcher. The Trooper was a very strong man but he struggled mightily to lift the heavy tube onto his right shoulder. As the rebels stood below, shocked by the sight of the awesome weapon, the Trooper took aim. Focused on aiming at the rebels, the Trooper didn't see the remaining Patriot guard sprinting at him from his right. The Patriot's shoulder hit the Trooper hard just under his outstretched arms.

With a hundred pounds of advanced weaponry on his

shoulder, the Trooper was extremely top-heavy. He hit the railing hard and tumbled over it, rocket launcher and all. As he hit the floor, the weapon discharged and a rocket streaked across the core into a brick wall. It easily penetrated the inside wall and opened a hole about eight feet in diameter in the outside wall of the building.

"Holy shit, that was close," Jimmy said to himself.

The Patriot soldier walked nervously down the stairs with his arms raised. He was well aware of the fact that over a dozen rebel guns were aimed at his chest. "I surrender! Don't shoot!" he said.

"Okay," Jimmy said pointing his gun at the Patriot. "Kristina, why don't you guard our new friend? Everyone else, start loading the truck and move quickly. We'll take what we can load into the truck in the next fifteen minutes. Then we leave. We can't risk that a call for help didn't get through to the outside. And it's possible that someone heard that rocket explosion even out here in the middle of nowhere."

At that moment, Stan walked out from his hiding place in the janitor's closet.

"Man, you guys made quite a racket!" he said laughingly, "I almost crapped when I heard that big explosion." He looked at the gaping hole in the wall and said, "Wow. That must have been what was in the Armageddon Cabinet."

While the other men were loading the truck, Jimmy carefully planted explosive charges around the inside of the armory. A half-hour from now, the armory would be a burned out, empty shell. Whatever weapons they weren't able to take, the explosives would render them useless.

The men were able to get at least three-quarters of the weaponry loaded. As they pulled away from the armory, Patrick asked Jimmy, "Where do we go from here?"

"We're heading back toward Newtown to drop off everyone but you, me, Mike, Jason and Kristina. We'll drop the other guys about a mile outside of the city, they can walk from there. The rest of us have a long night ahead helping Charlie unload the truck."

Suddenly there was a series of loud explosions. The armory building still stood, but flame and smoke poured out of the doors. The truck was already a quarter-mile away.

Jimmy said to Stan, "We can't thank you enough for your help. But you've put yourself into a bad situation. The Freedom Troopers will be checking the homes of everyone who was working at the armory tonight. As the only survivor you'll be under intense suspicion because they know the rebels had to have help from the inside. Even if you survive the questioning, you'll end up confessing. Your next stop would be a firing squad."

"I figured that," Stan answered, "my wife and kid are already at Charlie's house. As soon as I get back there, we're hitting the road. I have an old car, unregistered of course, and we should be able to get a couple hundred miles away by nightfall. I'll stay on the back roads just in case. We'll find a nice home to squat in and live underground."

"That's a good plan. You're a very brave man, and I wish you all the best," Jimmy said as he hugged Stan.

Then Jimmy moved over to where the Patriot soldier was sitting in a remote corner of trailer, still guarded by Kristina. Jimmy motioned for Kristina to move away and he put a pistol to the side of the man's head and said, "Convince me why I shouldn't shoot you right now. I'll give you two minutes."

Patrick couldn't hear the conversation, but it seemed to progress from contentious to somewhat cordial. Both men were talking and Jimmy was even laughing.

When the truck stopped to drop off most of the rebels, the Patriot soldier jumped off with them and stood on the side of the road, wondering which direction his home was in. Jimmy jumped off behind him. As the other rebels walked away, Jimmy quickly raised a pistol and shot the Patriot soldier twice through the head.

Patrick screamed, "Christ! Why did you do that? He saved our lives!"

Jimmy answered, "He did save us. That rocket would have wiped us all out. But he was the only soldier to survive the armory attack. How does that make him look? If that poor guy had gone home to his family like he was going to do, the Freedom Troopers would have picked him up by morning and 'debriefed' him until he was dead. And he would have told them everything about us. Believe me, he was better off with me shooting him. He was a dead man either way."

"If we do shit like that, we're no better than they are," Patrick said bitterly.

"Listen up everyone," Jimmy said loudly. "We aren't fucking heroes wearing white hats. We're in a battle for our lives. Sometimes we'll have to do ugly things that don't seem right. If we don't do those things, we won't survive. The rebellion is what matters. We'll do what it takes to win. If you can't live with that, then resign yourself to living the same shitty life you do now. Because things in this country won't get any better unless we do something about it."

The group rode silently to the warehouse, and few words were spoken as they unloaded the truck.

It was mid-morning by the time the truck was empty. As promised, Mark Johnson's friend had provided a large, secure room in a warehouse located just outside of Center City that was the perfect place to store the weapons.

The five rebels climbed into the back of the now-empty trailer. Charlie dropped them near Jimmy's car. They jammed into the sub-compact and rode back to Patrick's house, totally exhausted.

"Jimmy, stay with us for a couple of days," Kristina said. "You shouldn't be out. If they find you they'll surely bring you in for questioning." She ignored Patrick's glare. Obviously he was still upset with Jimmy for killing the Patriot soldier.

"I'm too tired to argue," Jimmy answered sleepily, "and you're right. We have to stay out sight for a couple of weeks. If you thought the government came down hard after our little ambush last month, wait until you see their reaction to this."

Entry Twelve: May 2025

Home from the armory attack, a tired group of rebels immediately collapsed into their beds and slept into the early evening. With the adrenalin drained from their systems, the exhilaration they felt several hours before turned into exhaustion and worry over what the government's reaction would be.

Patrick and Kristina woke up and immediately went to see who else was awake. They saw Jimmy, Maria and Megan sitting in the living room talking quietly.

"Patrick and Kristina," Jimmy said, "sit down and join us! I just woke up a while ago and was giving these two ladies the rundown on what happened last night."

"You guys did great!" Maria said as she got up and hugged both of them.

"I'm glad everybody made it back safely," Megan added.

"Everything went pretty much according to plan," Patrick said.

"We also got lucky," Jimmy said. "That Patriot soldier helped us when we really needed it." Jimmy told Megan and Maria the story of the rocket launcher and the Patriot soldier who saved them. "I know what I did seemed harsh. But there was no other way."

"I know," Patrick said, "I've given it a lot of thought in the past few hours. I understand your reasons, Jimmy. That doesn't stop me from feeling terrible about it."

As they were talking, Mike and Jason stumbled groggily into the living room and settled heavily into empty chairs. "You guys look awful," Maria said.

"I don't know about Jason, but I'm still exhausted. What time is it?" Mike said as he looked at a wall clock, "I'll be back in bed in a couple of hours."

"We need to talk about the future," Jimmy said, "we're going to have to make some changes in the way we're organized. Let me tell you what I have in mind."

"Is this the right time?" Kristina asked. "Can't it wait until tomorrow?"

"Let's talk about it tonight," Jimmy answered, "because we need to act fast and get this done tomorrow. Assuming you're all agreeable, of course."

"Sounds serious," Maria said.

"It is serious," Jimmy said. "Last night changes just about everything. For one, the government isn't going to give up their investigation after a few days like they did after the ambush four weeks ago. My guess is that several Freedom Troopers are on their way here now, and they'll try their best to make everyone's life in Newtown and Center City miserable."

"They didn't have any success last time finding out who did it," Megan said.

Jimmy responded, "That was nothing. They didn't even bring anyone in for interrogation last time. They just sent those idiots around town asking questions. I heard they concluded that it was a gang who carried out the ambush, not the rebels. This time it's obvious it was a rebel action and the investigation will be much more intense."

Maria asked, "What can we do?"

"I know you're not going to like this, but I think it's time for this household to go your separate ways. It's not safe for any of you here."

"No!" Megan cried, "I don't want to do that! This is where our life is! And how will we make a living? We have the farm here, there we have nothing."

"Don't worry," Jason told Megan, "we'll move south. That's where most of my family is. We can move in with them until we get things worked out."

"Our benefactor is willing to help you all," Jimmy said. "He'll give Megan and Maria both jobs in his company. Megan and Jason, you'll be moving south. You'll appear to be a nice young couple living happily as members of the Employed class. He'll set you up in housing there. Maria and Mike, you're moving west about a hundred miles. You'll also be an up-and-coming Employed couple; Maria will have a good job and will make enough money to allow Mike a lot of free time to work for the rebellion."

"What about us?" Kristina asked.

"You're leaving the area too," Jimmy said, "you're moving north to Center City. Patrick will be working for Mr. Johnson's company, a good job in sales. With that kind of job, he'll be able to travel around the area without being scrutinized. Being in the ranks of the Employed immediately gets you all off the radar as far as being suspects in the armory attack. But you have to split up and get out of the area. If you stay here you will be interrogated, probably in the next couple of days."

"What about you, Jimmy?" Patrick asked.

"I'm a hopeless case," Jimmy answered, "even if I had a job and Johnson tried to bury me somewhere in one of his companies, they would still find me. I would be arrested and interrogated. I need to go deep underground. Mark Johnson has set up a place for me to stay and will make sure that I have everything I need. But there's more to my plan than just running away from the government.

We're building momentum for the rebellion and we need some kind of structure."

Jimmy continued, "I'm still going to make the big picture strategic plans and determine where our attacks should take place. But each of you will be in charge of your sector. You'll be recruiting members and making all the tactical decisions: when to attack, how many men you'll need, how to carry out attacks and so forth. Doing it like this is the only way we're going to grow into a widespread rebellion."

Patrick said, "Speaking of strategy, have you thought about our next move?"

"I have a plan," Jimmy said, "we'll divide the weapons we took from the armory between us. We'll keep about half of them where they currently are, but each of you will get enough weapons to outfit about a hundred rebels. As soon as possible, I want you to organize guerilla attacks on Patriot Squads. We'll hit them by surprise and then disappear into the night. If we can pull off enough successful ambushes, we'll completely demoralize the Patriot Squads. When they had everybody under their thumb, those clods thought it was cool to make a few extra bucks and play at being big, important soldiers. We'll see how dedicated they are when they start going to funerals for their buddies every other week."

Jason said, "So our job will be to recruit about a hundred rebels in our areas. Then we train them, arm them and then pick our spots to attack the Patriot Squads. Is that right?"

"You got it," Jimmy answered. "You don't need a hundred recruits at first; get a few reliable ones to start. I know you all can do this, and I'm counting on you."

Everyone breathed a sigh of relief. In about ten minutes, they had gone from being homeless fugitives to having jobs and being rebel leaders.

Everyone went back to sleep a few hours later and slept soundly through the night. When Patrick woke up early the next morning, Jimmy and his car were already gone. He left a note that simply said, "You're all moving today. Pack your stuff. Wait to be contacted. I'll be in touch soon."

Entry Thirteen: May 2025

First Lieutenant Henry Greenwell was the commanding military officer for the area that included Center City and Newtown. To say he was having a bad day was an understatement. He had been up since the day before, when he was jarred awake by a call telling him that the armory had been cleaned out and destroyed.

When he got the call, Henry threw on his uniform and hopped into the Jeep that was parked in his driveway. As he drove toward the armory, he called the Regional Commander. This would be a highly unpleasant conversation and the longer he waited, the worse it would be. "Sir, I just received word there was an attack at the armory near Center City."

"Is everything all right? I assume the rebels were turned back," the Commander said.

"I'm on my way to assess the damage," Greenwell answered, "but I was told that the armory was taken by the rebels."

"Taken? What the fuck does that mean?"

"The rebels overcame the guards, sir. They were reportedly able to take a large number of weapons."

"Christ on a cross! Get over there, Greenwell, and contact me with a full and accurate report ASAP. Got it?"

"Yes sir," Henry answered and hung up.

As Henry Greenwell drove closer to the armory, he saw the gaping hole in the side of the building and knew at once that the situation was beyond even his worst fears. One area leader had arrived earlier after receiving a call from a resident living over a mile away who heard the explosion; the area leader was the one who called Henry. Six other area leaders plus a dozen Freedom Troopers were arriving just as he did. They got out of their vehicles and all stood staring at the exterior of the building, as if looking at it would un-do the damage.

"Let's go in. Weapons drawn," Lieutenant Greenwell ordered as he led the way.

Inside, the walls were charred and blackened. Bodies littered the floor of the central area. "Jerry," Henry said to one of his area leaders, "take an inventory of the remaining weapons. It looks to me like they got almost all of them. Also give me an assessment as to whether any weapons are salvageable or if they are damaged beyond repair."

"They look like piles of scrap metal to me," Jerry said.

"I said to make a formal report, you idiot! I don't want your opinion, I want the weapons counted, inspected and assessed for damage," Greenwell screamed, and then turned to the group of men. "This is an example of where our complacency about the rebels has gotten us! It's a good thing these guards are dead, or they would be shot right here on the spot for dereliction of duty!" To make his point, he took out his pistol and put two rounds into the body of one of the dead guards.

Another area leader spoke up, "Sir, my men and I will take a body count and identify the dead. There is a possibility that some of the guards deserted."

"If any guards did run away, I pity them," Greenwell said icily, "they will be severely punished." He turned to another area leader and said, "Organize your men to question everyone within a mile radius of this facility. Find out if anyone heard or saw anything. Have a report to me by 1500 hours today."

Another area leader was ordered to take a group of Freedom Troopers to visit the residence of all guards and civilian employees who were on duty the night of the attack. Greenwell barked, "If any of them are in their homes, arrest them immediately and bring them in for interrogation. The rebels got assistance from someone on the inside. My guess is that whoever is still alive was the one who helped them."

It was time to call the Commander. He pushed a few buttons on his cellular phone. "Sir, this is Lieutenant Greenwell. I have bad news regarding the armory. My inspection indicates that three-quarters or more of the weapons stored there have been removed. I have a man inspecting the remaining weapons, but on first inspection it appears they are no longer usable."

Several minutes of screaming, cursing and explaining followed. The last thing the Regional Commander screamed was that he was sending in "a specialist in rebel control" to take over command of the sector, and that Henry would be reassigned to other duties effective the first of July.

Entry Fourteen: May 2025

It was a bittersweet day for Patrick's household. While Maria and Kristina were packing their small amount of belongings in cardboard boxes, Maria said, "It's sad to leave here, but I'm excited for us to be moving. We'll be closer to Michael's family so he will be happy about that."

"I feel the same way," Kristina said, "the six of us have been working and living together for three years. You could not have been a better friend, Maria. I'm sad to part ways, but I agree with Jimmy. They'll bring every suspected rebel in for interrogation within a few days, and you can be sure that some – or all – of us are on that list."

"You don't have to work, which will be nice. It will be different for me to have a real job – I've never had one before."

"You'll do just fine at it," Kristina reassured her, "I'm sure that I'll keep busy. Maybe we'll have a little land and I can plant a garden." Kristina's strong suit in the household was her knowledge and enthusiasm about farming their vegetable crop.

"The men are excited because it's a big step forward for the rebellion. I heard Patrick, Jason and Michael talking about strategy on how they plan to recruit members in their areas."

"I don't think they'll have a problem with recruiting. There are a lot of people who are just sitting back, waiting for the opportunity to join the rebellion."

Patrick walked into the room and asked, "How is the packing coming along?"

"Fine," Kristina answered, "We'll be ready to go within ten minutes."

"Good. The longer we stay, the more dangerous it is."

Kristina said, "I feel terrible leaving all of those crops out there to rot. Couldn't we tell our neighbors that they can harvest the crops?"

"Absolutely not," Patrick said. "If the Freedom Troopers come around and our neighbors tell them that we moved away, they'll figure out that we were involved in the armory attack. Then they won't give up until they find us. We need to just disappear."

"Won't the government be able to track us down, since we'll have jobs and houses?" Maria asked.

"Mr. Johnson is faking our government ID cards; basically

he's creating new identities for us. It's not foolproof, but unless the government knows what direction we went, they won't be able to find us. And the fact we're splitting up will confuse them even more."

At that moment, a small van stopped in front of the house and the driver approached the front door. Patrick froze and whispered, "Be very quiet. I'll answer the door. Be ready to slip out the back if it sounds like trouble."

Patrick opened the door cautiously and said, "Can I help you?"

"Hello," the man said, "I'm from Johnson Mining and Industrial. I was sent here to pick up six people and some boxes. Are you ready to go?"

"Give us a few minutes," Patrick said. "Wait in the van."

The six housemates stood silently in the living room, their meager possessions contained in a dozen small boxes by the front door.

"This is it, everybody..." Patrick's voice cracked. The six exchanged tearful hugs, picked up their boxes and walked out the door to their new lives.

Entry Fifteen: June 2025

Henry Greenwell read over the final report before he emailed it to the Regional Commander. It did not paint a pretty picture. The weapons that the rebels left behind couldn't be salvaged and the structural integrity of the building was completely ruined by the rocket explosion.

Since the armory served eight sectors (an area about the size of New York state) there was going to be an extreme shortage of weapons and ammunition for the next several months. At a time and place when rebel activity was at a peak, the Freedom Troopers would have to ration their ammunition.

With weapons in short supply, the Patriot Squads would be required to give up their guns to the professional troops who were flooding into the sector. Whoever came up with the idea of Patriot Squads is the one who should be punished, Henry thought bitterly. The reason he was in this mess was that some General in Washington decided to give those low-grade morons the responsibility of guarding the armory.

Henry had just learned a few hours before that he was being transferred to oversee a remote area in what used to be West Texas. The weather was hotter than shit and the rebels down there were a rough bunch of drug dealers with no fear of authority. The rumor was that his predecessor's severed head was found mounted on a stick in the desert a few weeks earlier. He shivered involuntarily and cursed out loud as he sent the email.

**

It took Patrick less than two weeks to organize his first rebel action. The Freedom Troopers had flocked to Center City and Newtown in imposing numbers since the armory attack. But even with more soldiers, they needed to concentrate their efforts on keeping order in the more lawless urban areas. Patrols at the edges of the city were still being done by Patriot Squads. Because of the shortage of weapons, only about half the men in a Patriot Squad carried a full complement of weapons. The other men were there for appearance only.

Having taken a few days to observe the Patriot Squads moving about the outskirts of Center City, Patrick formulated a plan to ambush them. He also spent a great deal of time circulating among the unemployed lower class, probing people he talked to in order to gauge their interest in the rebellion. There were three men that he selected to join him on the first mission.

He asked the new recruits to meet with him at the house

that he lived in with Kristina. The house was similar in size to the one he shared with five other people in Newtown, and Patrick was still getting used to the feeling of living in what felt like a cavernous, empty home.

"You need to be prepared for bloodshed," Patrick warned the men. "Our objective is to instill fear in the Patriot Squads. The way to do that is to make a strong statement on this first attack. Do you understand what I'm saying?"

All three men nodded.

After he laid out the plan, Patrick asked, "Are you guys ready for this?" Without hesitation, all answered that they were.

"All right then. Let's go downstairs to the basement. We'll go over how the guns and other weapons work. We obviously can't do any practice shooting, but we'll handle the guns and get an idea of how they feel."

The training session went very well, and Patrick reviewed the plan once again before the men left the house. They agreed to meet the next night at 9 p.m.

***

As instructed, the three men arrived precisely on time and all were wearing dark clothes with black knit caps.

"Do we need to cover our faces?" one man asked Patrick.

"We're not going to leave any witnesses, so don't bother," Patrick answered flatly.

Patrick had tracked one of the Patriot Squads that patrolled the edge of Center City and determined the perfect spot for an ambush. A pedestrian tunnel about sixty feet long ran under a road, and the Patriot goons walked through the tunnel at about the same time each night as they followed their usual route.

"When the men in the front are about ten feet from the end of the tunnel, you two step in front of them and start shooting," Patrick said, "Blast away, shoot as fast as you can. Their reaction will be to retreat back through the tunnel. Follow them in and force them in that direction."

Patrick motioned toward one of his men and continued, "The two of us will be waiting for them at the back end, on either side of the tunnel entrance. Whoever you don't get, we'll pick them off as they come out of the tunnel. Just make sure no one gets out of your end alive."

The Patriot Squad showed up right on schedule and entered the tunnel. Patrick waited patiently for the sound of gunfire. When the shooting started, he motioned to the rebel on the other side of the tunnel entrance to get ready to fire. Of the twenty Patriot soldiers who entered the tunnel, six were still uninjured by the initial flurry of gunfire and came running out the back end. One by one, Patrick aimed and fired his rifle. His partner shot two soldiers and Patrick shot the other four.

Once the shooting ceased and all twenty Patriot soldiers were down, Patrick said, "Now we have to finish them." He led his group around to the soldiers and shot each once in the head. A few were still moving and groaning, but thankfully none of them were aware of the final shot.

The group of men walked quietly about a block to a pre-determined meeting place, and moments later Kristina pulled up in Patrick's car. They all piled in.

The new rebels were extremely boisterous. "Wow! That was amazing!" one said.

"It went perfectly. Good job, everyone," Patrick said. "I need to caution you...don't talk about this to anyone. Not even your family." The men nodded their agreement.

Kristina dropped each of the men at their homes. With Patrick now alone in the car, she asked, "Did the mission really go as well as you said?"

"Yeah, it did. It was almost too easy. Half those Patriots didn't even have guns. Now that we've exposed our-selves, they'll be much more careful on their patrols. The next attack will be harder, you can count on that."

Entry Sixteen: June 2025

The entrance door to the dark, empty retail store opened with a squeak, and Patrick saw Jason and Mike enter tentatively, squinting in the darkness for anyone else who might be there. Jimmy had contacted the three of them to arrange a meeting to share their experiences ambushing Patriot Squads.

Patrick smiled and hugged Mike, then Jason. "Man, it's good to see you guys! Jimmy isn't here yet. No one saw you come in here, did they?"

"All clear," Mike answered. "I don't think anyone has set foot near this shopping center in years. The parking lot is practically all weeds."

At that moment, Jimmy came in and motioned everyone to the rear of the store. "I picked this place because I've never seen anyone around here," Jimmy said, "but it doesn't hurt to be careful and stay in the back, away from the windows. So, let's talk. I've heard all three of you have carried out a successful ambush. Tell me about it."

Patrick talked about his success recruiting rebels and told the story of his attack, then Mike and Jason related similar experiences. In all three attacks, the rebels suffered no casualties and had totally wiped out the Patriot Squads that they targeted.

After they discussed the attacks, Jimmy said, "Say, have you all heard about the government scheduling elections for this fall? That's the latest information from my sources. They're supposedly going to announce it next week, on Independence Day."

"Why would they do that?" Patrick asked, "Why should they risk their position of power when they know that they're hated?"

"From what I heard, they feel the need to calm the citizenry and give the impression that the people are in charge. There are rebels operating all around the country; momentum is starting to build and the government is getting nervous. Of course, the elections will be fixed, there's no question about that. They've been manipulating elections since 2012," Jimmy answered.

"How could that possibly have happened? Wouldn't that be very difficult to do?" Mike asked.

Jimmy went into what Patrick called "professor mode," and started to lecture, "There have always been charges of fixing elections throughout the history of the country. What happened starting in about 2009 couldn't really be called fixing elections; it was more changing the entire system to stack the odds in the favor of the right-wing extremists who were trying to seize power. You see, the more people who voted, the less chance the right-wing extremists stood of be elected. Their supporters were a relatively small group, but very vocal and very committed to their cause. The 2008 Presidential election drove the extremists crazy – regular people voted in big numbers and their guy lost. So the right-wingers started systematically taking steps to keep many people from being eligible to vote."

"That doesn't seem possible. How could they do that?" Jason said skeptically.

"The extremists claimed that there was rampant voter fraud and used that as an excuse to change the laws to exclude people from voting. For example, many states passed laws requiring that a person have a government photo ID in order to vote. That one step eliminated about one-fifth of voters – the poor, elderly without driver's licenses, many young people – they couldn't vote."

"But don't you think there may have actually been voter fraud?" Jason asked.

"Here's a few statistics for you," Jimmy lectured. "Out of *300 million votes* cast between 2002 and 2007, the U.S. Justice Department had a grand total of *eighty-six* convictions for voter fraud. And there were *zero* convictions for impersonating a voter, which is the main reason a photo ID would be important. In one state, Wisconsin, they tried like hell to find voter fraud and came up with a grand total of seven one-hundredths of one percent that were even classified as suspicious."

Jimmy continued, "The thing was, it was a systematic effort, being carried out by a group funded by a couple of billionaires named David and Charles Koch. These guys were the ones who bankrolled the right-wing extremists in the first place, and then they changed the rules so their candidates would win."

"Maybe this election will be different," Mike said hopefully.

"Not a chance," Jimmy answered, "they'll use the whole government ID requirement again and that will eliminate nearly half the people from voting. Do any of you three guys have government ID cards?"

Jason and Mike shook their heads. Mike said, "Of course, Maria and Megan have ID cards because you need one to have a job."

Patrick said, "I had to get one to have a job, but Mr. Johnson set me up with one that has a phony name."

"So the Wealthy and the Employed will be able to vote, but hardly anyone else. How do you think the Wealthy and Employed will vote?"

The question hung in the air, because the answer was obvious. The three young men gave up on the discussion.

When Jimmy was on a roll, there was no room for differences of opinion.

"Okay," Patrick said, "what's the next step then, Jimmy?"

"I'd like to see you continue the ambushes, but we need to be much more careful. Stick to the attacks at bridges and tunnels; that strategy has been working great. There are two or three times as many Freedom Troopers in the area than there were a month ago. When you ambush a Patriot Squad, they'll probably have Freedom Troopers with them. That makes things more difficult and dangerous. Make sure your attacks are planned extremely well, don't try any seat-of-the-pants bullshit."

"You don't have to tell us that, Jimmy," Mike said, "I've seen the Freedom Troopers marching. We need to take them seriously."

Jimmy said, "Also, the Independence Day celebrations are coming up in a few days. I've heard rumors that there will be demonstrations. Obviously, those people who protest are important to the overall goal, but they have nothing to do with our activities. Don't get involved in that stuff. All those demonstrators will be face-scanned by government cameras and put on file as possible rebels. It's important for us to stay anonymous. The guys that report to you should stay away from those demonstrations, too. Tell them not to even go to the government-sanctioned events. It just isn't worth the risk."

All three men agreed and Jimmy wrapped up the meeting. The men left the shopping center one-by-one and headed for their respective homes.

Entry Seventeen: July 2025

Patrick met the following day with his volunteers and cautioned them against attending the Independence Day celebrations. One of the rebels took vocal exception.

"Listen, Patrick," he said, "my family is looking forward to going to the parade and the band concert at Memorial Park in Center City. That's a big family event for us. I was even thinking of carrying a sign. You know, we still have free speech in this country."

"Come on, Steve," Patrick argued. "First, to say we have free speech is bullshit. The lower class doesn't have much to lose so we can be more vocal. But speak up and you'll be harassed by Patriot Squad goons, maybe hauled in for questioning and beat up. How much freedom is that?"

Another volunteer chimed in to support Patrick, "The Wealthy and Employed know enough to keep quiet. If they spoke up they'd find out pretty quickly how much 'freedom' they really have – they would lose everything if they said what they really thought."

"I'm just tired of sitting around. Carrying a sign is better than doing nothing," Steve complained, "we've had one ambush in the past three weeks. That pace is getting us nowhere."

"We're all frustrated," Patrick said, "But we have to be smart and pick our spots carefully. I'm telling you, don't go to the celebration. You can't afford to be face-scanned. Even if you just attend and don't protest, if there's trouble you could end up getting dragged into it. Secrecy is our biggest advantage and having you on file as a potential rebel would endanger all of us."

With three intense faces staring at him, Steve knew he was on the losing side of the argument. He said reluctantly, "I'll talk to my wife and kids about it. They won't be happy."

"In the meantime," Patrick said as brightly as he could, "I've come up with a plan for an attack that we can do tomorrow night. If you want, Steve, we can leave a sign there that this was our Independence Day celebration." Patrick laid out his plan and asked the rebels, "Are you in?"

All three volunteers nodded enthusiastically.

***

Lieutenant Greenwell finished packing his desk and looked around one last time at the now-barren walls of his office. This was the best assignment he had in his five-year military career. The weather was decent and, until recently, rebel activity was fairly tame compared to some other parts of the country. That was the problem – in spite of Greenwell's continuous pleas to his troops, they fell into a state of complacency that culminated in the embarrassing armory attack by the rebels.

After that goddamned fiasco, there was no stopping the course of events that led to his transfer. After he spent a few hours briefing his replacement, the Lieutenant would go home to his wife and little girl, finish packing their possessions and start the two-day drive to his new assignment in Texas. He heard a rumor that several members of his staff had started a macabre office pool to bet on the number of months before Greenwell would be killed by the rebels down there and in what manner they would kill him.

His thoughts were interrupted by the opening of his office door. Blocking practically the entire space of the doorway was one of the most massive and imposing figures Greenwell had ever seen. The top of the man's head was a couple of inches away from grazing the top of the frame as he stood at near-attention. His broad shoulders were bolstered by heavy padding, but the width of his shoulders nearly touched both sides of the doorway. He wore a dress uniform that was decorated with more medals than Greenwell could count, topped off with a dress hat and aviator sunglasses.

"I'm Colonel Victor Nefario," the man said in a booming voice. "You must be Greenwood."

"Green*well*, sir. I just finished packing. Please, sit down; I've prepared a briefing for you on the situation here."

Nefario laughed, "I won't require any briefing, Lieutenant. I'm fully aware of the state of this region, thank you. You're dismissed." The Colonel motioned to three junior officers that were hidden behind his immense figure, and they quickly carried boxes into the office, brushing by Greenwell as if he wasn't there.

"Well...then," Greenwell stammered, "I suppose I'll be leaving." Nefario ignored him and started pointing to various cabinets and barking orders to his assistants.

It took less than a half-hour for any trace of the previous occupant to be erased from the offices. The three junior officers efficiently removed all files from the storage cabinets and packed them neatly in boxes. Three modest desks were installed in the outer office, one for each assistant. The Colonel unpacked a very small box of personal items and arranged them on his desk, which took about ten seconds. Victor Nafario was not a sentimental man and had no family that anyone was aware of.

After the junior officers were finished scurrying about, Nefario sent all but one of them home for the evening. It had been a long drive in a packed military vehicle from Washington D.C. and the Colonel was in an even surlier mood than usual. He asked his most-trusted junior officer, Sergeant Rick Randall, to mix them both a whiskey and water.

Nefario took a swig of his drink and hissed loudly. "Well, here we are, Rick. This assignment is a disgrace. How in the fuck did I ever fall to this sorry place in my career?"

"It isn't so bad," Randall said with as much enthusiasm as he could. After years as the Colonel's trusted aide, Rick Randall knew Nefario was subject to periods of intense melancholy. He would be as encouraging as possible to his commander, but secretly he doubted that the Colonel would be able to bear the humiliation attached to his demotion and this assignment.

"Fuck you and your optimism. The way I've been treated is bullshit! Six months ago I was *General* Nefario. I commanded the military effort for nearly a third of the entire country!"

"I know, sir. But it's not uncommon in military history for great leaders to be demoted. The strong ones come back and claim their glory. And you're one of the strong ones."

The comment seemed to defuse some of the Colonel's anger. "You're right. But you and I both know I was treated shabbily. I was ordered to maintain control of my area, and I did so. Admittedly, some of my actions were a bit brutal – but in my judgment, I did exactly what was needed."

"It was really the fault of your superiors, sir. They failed to communicate clearly the limits of force that you were authorized to use."

"Fucking-aye right," Nefario said as he raised his glass toward Rick Randall. "Yes, I ordered a massive bombing of a known rebel area. I figured out where they were and sent a couple of cruise missiles right up their asses."

"We wiped out a hundred rebels in one swipe," Randall said.

"But then my superiors turned on me. 'Oh, you destroyed a hospital! Innocent lives were lost!' They acted like the bunch of faggots they are. The rebels were hiding there because they figured the government wouldn't have the balls to bomb a hospital. Well, fuck that. We got them and we also got rid of those sympathizer doctors who conspired to let them use the hospital as a rebel headquarters."

"Those doctors would have been in front of a firing squad a few weeks later anyway," Randall agreed.

"And who cares about the patients who were killed?" Nefario said bitterly, "Most of them were low-class charity cases anyway. We did the country a favor and thinned the herd."

"Thinning the herd" was one of the Colonel's favorite expressions and he always followed it with a derisive laugh.

The Sergeant didn't want to spoil Nefario's improved mood, so he stopped himself from talking about the aftermath of the hospital attack. Instead of being grateful for a major victory in what was perhaps the strongest pocket of rebels in the nation, the politicians accused General Nefario of igniting greater revolutionary fervor and strengthening the rebellion. True, the hundred rebels that were killed in the hospital bombing were replaced by several hundred new ones, according to the figures cited at the Colonel's disciplinary hearing. But the new rebels were untrained and disorganized. Nefario remained convinced that the bombing was effective and had set back the rebellion by months, if not years.

His opinion was a minority of one, however, and Victor Nefario was stripped of his command, demoted to Colonel and assigned to a desk job in the Pentagon for several months. This was his first field assignment since the hospital bombing.

As if he was reading his assistant's thoughts, Nefario said, "Those fucking politicians. They wanted us to quell the rebellion, but then they drew some invisible line that we weren't allowed to cross. This is war! There are no limits in war, especially ones that are set by whore politicians."

Randall knew very well from experience that the Colonel's dark moods were capable of keeping the Sergeant trapped in this office listening to him wallow in self-pity for the next several hours. Trying to recapture the positive mood of a few minutes before, Randall said, "We need to look at this assignment as an opportunity. You can prove yourself again. You've done it many times before."

Colonel Nefario was given a Regional Command, unlike the unfortunate Henry Greenwell, who only commanded an area, the equivalent of less than one state. Under a plan Nefario himself had promoted, there were five regions in what were formerly the forty-eight states. Nefario's region was called the "Near West" and covered an area from Montana, Wyoming and Colorado in the west across to Wisconsin and Illinois in the eastern part of the region. On the surface, it seemed like a terrible region and the higher-ups thought they were punishing Nefario by sending him there. They didn't realize that the Near West region contained the final piece that would allow him to implement his plan.

Nefario reflected for a few moments, "You're absolutely right. Just between you and me, Rick, I do have a plan for a comeback. I'm not ready to talk about it yet, even with you. But believe me, if I can pull it off we'll be bigger than ever before. Being a General again is nothing compared to where I plan to be. Until then, I have some ideas on how to take care of the rebels in this area that we'll start tomorrow. You can call it a night, Rick. I'm going to stay for a while and get some papers organized. But before you go, pray with me."

After he completed a short prayer and his junior officer left, Colonel Nefario leaned back and put his feet on the desk. His mind played out what he hoped to accomplish in the next few months.

Something he didn't tell Rick Randall (or anyone else)

was that the Supreme Commander, none other than the nation's head military man, had a very private conversation with Nefario just the day before. The Colonel was given this assignment for a reason, he was told by the General, because he had proven himself to possess the ruthlessness that was called for in this situation.

The rebels in the region were bolder and more successful than had been seen in other areas of the country. With a huge stockpile of the latest weapons, there was a real danger that the rebellion in this region could gain some traction and become a serious threat. Strong measures were needed, and an example needed to be made that unlawful revolt would not be tolerated.

Colonel Nefario had absolutely no hesitation to shed all the blood that was necessary to put an end to the rebellion. He likened the rebels to insects – they were pests, parasites on society who did nothing but use valuable resources that should be reserved for those who actually contributed to society. They were Godless and without morals, and they deserved to be slaughtered.

Entry Eighteen: July 2025

"I don't care what your friend Patrick says, we're going to the Independence Day celebration. It's a family tradition!"

Steve knew his wife would put up a fight about not attending the holiday festivities. Although he didn't fully agree with the reasons and really wanted to take his family, Steve decided to go along with Patrick's request. "I know; it's something we've done every year since the girls were born. How about if just you and the kids go? I'll stay home."

"Absolutely not!" his wife said. "It's a day for family. That means all four of us. Plus, this may be the last Independence Day celebration. You know the government is talking about changing Independence Day to 'Constitution Day' or something like that."

"Yeah, I know. The government prefers to celebrate the date that the new government repealed the Seventeenth Amendment, the one that allows the people to elect Senators. The same day they revised Section III and allowed

Congress to fire Supreme Court justices at will, and also the same day they added the Amendment that defined marriage as only between a man and woman of the same race, and another Amendment that abolished legal abortion." Steve hoped getting his wife into a fiery political discussion would disarm her anger about not going to the celebration, but no luck.

"That makes it even more important that we go. Don't you want the girls to remember Independence Day?"

"Patrick said there's very likely going to be trouble there, and I don't want to become involved in it. Things have been going well lately and I don't want to get in bad with the government."

"Since when did you become such a wimp? You used to be outspoken about what you thought about the government."

Steve was beginning to see the next twenty-four hours play out in front of him. There would be another few hours of arguing and he would either eventually give into her or get the silent treatment for the next week. There was a third alternative, and that was the one he chose – give in to her right away and enjoy the holiday.

"All right," he said wearily, "But no protesting of any sort – no signs, no t-shirts with anti-government slogans, nothing like that. We go and sit quietly and enjoy ourselves."

His wife gave him a hug and said, "Of course, sweetheart. We'll have a great time as usual."

"I'm going to hang out with Patrick tonight, but I'll be home as early as early as I can. We'll head into Center City at about noon. OK?" As far as his wife was concerned, Steve and Patrick were buddies who liked to go out for a beer now and then. She was far too volatile and outspoken for Steve to trust her with the fact that he was active in the rebellion, and that tonight he was going to participate in an ambush.

Entry Nineteen: July 2025

Jason and his small team of rebels were also planning an ambush on the eve of Independence Day. Jason had been shadowing a Patriot Squad for the past week and they looked ripe for the picking. Their route required them to cross a river over a footbridge that was about forty yards long.

The plan called for two rebels to be stationed on one end of the bridge and two to hide at the other end. Once the Patriot Squad was in the middle of the span, the four men would attack them from both ends of the bridge and wipe them out. Jason, Patrick and Mike had all used what Jimmy called the "bridge and tunnel strategy" on their first attacks and they had gone flawlessly. Jimmy suggested to all three leaders that they should stick with the same strategy, since it had been so successful the first time.

At about 10 p.m. the four men settled into their hiding places and checked their weapons. If they stayed true to their schedule, the Patriot Squad would approach the bridge within the next half hour.

"Here they come!" Jason put down his night goggles and whispered into a walkie-talkie as he saw the soldiers appear about fifty yards from the bridge. "This will be even easier than I thought – there aren't any Freedom Troopers with them like there've been for the past week!"

Within a minute, the twenty government soldiers were all on the bridge and Jason gave the order to attack. A moment after the rebels jumped out of hiding, two dozen Freedom Troopers appeared from the woods surrounding the bridge and moved quickly toward Jason and his fellow rebels. Instead of the Patriot Squad, it was the rebels that were caught in a deadly crossfire. The soldiers on the bridge quickly split into two groups, each attacking the rebels at either end. In the meantime, the Freedom Troopers were behind the rebels, cutting off any chance of retreat.

With the rebels badly outnumbered and the element of surprise lost, the battle was over quickly. Within a few minutes, Jason and the other three rebels were dead on the ground.

A military vehicle pulled up ten minutes later and Colonel Nefario jumped out of the passenger seat. He surveyed the area, making a point to kick each of the bodies as he walked past them.

"Who was in charge of this operation?" Nefario asked brusquely.

"I planned the operation, sir," answered one of the Freedom Troopers.

"No, Corporal. *I* planned it. You simply followed orders. All three of the previous ambushes on Patriot Squads took place on bridges or in a tunnel. It wasn't difficult to surmise that the rebels would try the same thing again, and I ordered Freedom Troopers to hide at all bridges and tunnels. But you executed the plan perfectly, Corporal. I'll make sure this goes into your permanent record."

"Thank you, sir. I appreciate that."

Nefario turned to his driver, "Sergeant Randall, make sure that we search each of those bodies thoroughly. None of them will have an ID, but find out whatever you can. Put pictures of the infidels on posters and offer a reward for any information about their identities. If we figure out who they are or where they live, that could lead us to the other rebels."

Entry Twenty: July 2025

Fortunately, Patrick decided to go against Jimmy's advice and alter his strategy from the first attack. He chose not to attack a Patriot Squad at a bridge or tunnel. For this ambush, he and his men were going to attack a Treatment Center.

Starting in 2018, the government established "Treatment Centers" where gay men and women were housed for rehabilitation. The patients received psychological counseling and various undefined treatments that generally lasted twelve to eighteen months. The program was designed for the Wealthy and Employed, and although participation was not mandated by law, any Wealthy or Employed household that did not place a known gay family member in the program faced intense scrutiny from the government and from their peers. The program had excellent results, although the treated patients tended to not be highly functional after they were discharged.

The plan was to break into the Treatment Center, menace the staff and perhaps free a handful of patients who were eager to leave. Patrick had observed the place to be well-guarded and the primary goal was to discourage the medical people who staffed the centers from working there. Patrick counted on a hard fight from the perimeter Freedom Trooper guards.

Since Colonel Nefario had ordered most of the Freedom Troopers away from their regular duties to watch bridges and tunnels, the Treatment Center was guarded by a small crew that evening. The four rebels easily crept to the wire fence and cut a large hole in it. They ran toward the large brick building, completely undetected in the darkness.

The Treatment Center looked very much like a public school that Patrick remembered attending in his youth. It was mostly brick, with many windows and glass doors. The rebels tried one of the secondary doors and found it to be locked, so Patrick broke the glass door with his rifle butt and opened the door from the inside. A few moments later a loud, piercing alarm began blaring.

"Head toward the front of the building! Follow me this way!" Patrick said.

As the rebels ran down the wide corridor, they were met by two pudgy security guards, both brandishing pistols. The four rebels stopped and raised their rifles, and the security guards quickly turned and scurried the other way. The rebels continued down the hall until they arrived at a large open area that looked like a reception area. There were no staff members present.

"Uh, oh," Patrick said, "If the staff has all gone into hiding that probably means they've called for help. We've only got a couple of minutes." Suddenly, Patrick regretted his choice of target. If the Freedom Troopers arrived before they were able to get out, they could surround the perimeter of the facility and the rebels would be trapped.

Patrick looked around. Behind the reception desk was a sturdy, metal door. He tried it and found it locked. He shouted through the door, "I'm counting to three and then putting a grenade by this door. Either unlock it for me or step back and take cover, although you'll probably be blown up anyway. All right...One, two, three!"

The door popped open. Inside were two security people looking at a console that included a bank of monitor screens and countless switches.

As the rebels pointed their rifles at the two guards, Patrick examined the electronic control board and shouted, "Do these switches open the patient room doors?"

The security guard paused for a few seconds while considering his options. "Yes," he answered hesitantly. It wasn't part of the plan, but suddenly Patrick had an inspiration. What better way to wreak havoc than to let all the patients free?

"Open all of them!" Patrick yelled. He and the rebels began throwing switches as fast as they could. "Go down the halls and wake all the patients! But hurry, we need to be outside in sixty seconds!"

The rebels each ran down a corridor, screaming for the patients to leave the building and run. About a hundred residents poured into the hallways and out the front entrance. Fortunately, the Freedom Troopers had yet to arrive, and the rebels led the group through the opening in the fence. There were stragglers among the patients, and many were either unwilling or unable to leave the facility. There was no time to answer questions or explain – the patients either chose to dash for an uncertain freedom or face continued "treatment" if they stayed behind.

After they all got through the fence, Patrick led the mass of people into the woods adjacent to the grounds. They stopped and quietly watched the arrival of three dozen Freedom Troopers, who surrounded the building and entered from various sides.

Now that he had let them out, what could Patrick do with all of these people?

"Okay, everyone. Follow us through the woods. We need to put some distance between us and those Freedom Troopers. And keep quiet!"

Waiting at the back edge of the woods in Patrick's car was Kristina, who expected to pick up Patrick and his three rebel friends. Instead she saw nearly a hundred gown-clad patients.

Patrick recalled that they were only a couple of miles from the abandoned shopping mall. He said to the patients, "Up this road a couple of miles there's an abandoned strip shopping center. I'll lead you, so stay right behind me. You'll sleep there tonight. Tomorrow we'll get you food and water."

Patrick sent his three rebels home to their families, while he led the patients through the wooded area along the road to the shopping center. Then he and Kristina stayed up all night guarding the patients who were now sleeping in the rear of the stores. They made sure there were absolutely no lights on in the building and hid their car a mile away. A large military vehicle packed with Freedom Troopers passed by the shopping center but didn't even slow down. The hiding place turned out to be a perfect choice, with weeds overgrowing the parking lot, several cracked and broken windows, and heavy vines crawling up the outside walls. It looked like no human had set foot in there for years.

The next morning before dawn, Patrick gathered the patients and gave them instructions.

"You're all free," he explained, "but that freedom comes with a price. You have two choices. You can return home to your families, and chances are they'll send you right back to a Treatment Center. Your second choice is to become a member of the underclass."

He followed this with a half-hour lecture on how to select a house to squat in, where to find food, and other information on how to survive as a member of the underclass.

As he talked, he sensed that several patients would probably not be able to make it on their own and return home or be captured.

When he finished his lecture, one of the patients raised his hand. He said, "There's a third option you didn't mention. Perhaps you could use our help in the resistance." The comment was met by applause and cheers by many of the patients.

"Good idea," Patrick answered, "but there are a lot of details that need to be taken care of to make that possible. How are we going to feed and clothe nearly a hundred people?"

"Let us stay here and get us enough food and water for a few days. We'll help you figure it out."

"All right. Kristina will go get more food and water right now. You and I will be in charge of the group," Patrick said to the patient who had spoken up. "No one is to leave here. If you do, you will most certainly be arrested, interrogated to within an inch of your life, and sent back to the Treatment Center. Do not leave the building except to go in back and take care of your personal business. You'll be safe here."

As she was leaving, Patrick said to Kristina, "I'm beginning to think this wasn't a good idea. This is going to be like herding cats. If any of them leave and get picked up, there'll be Freedom Troopers here within minutes."

"I wouldn't worry too much," Kristina said, "they have nowhere to go. They don't know where they are. I don't think any of them will be wandering off. But keep an eye on them."

"Maybe this will work. They were all pretty disoriented and many of them were drugged up. My guess is they'll sleep most of the day."

Entry Twenty-One: July 2025

About midday, Patrick awoke from his sound but uncomfortable sleep on the floor to loud pounding on the front window of the storefront. He peeked out to see Jimmy standing there. "Let me in!" Jimmy said urgently.

Jimmy burst through the front door the moment Patrick cracked it open. "What the fuck are you doing? I just stopped by your house and Kristina told me about your idiotic plan!"

"Settle down," Patrick said, "it's under control."

"Bullshit. If one of these patients walks out of here or gets picked up, it will fuck up everything that we've accomplished. This is a really stupid thing you've done."

Patrick rubbed his eyes and said, "Why are you here?"

"I have very bad news. Jason was killed last night, along with the three guys that were with him. They walked into a trap. You're lucky the same thing didn't happen to you."

Patrick sat quiet and half-dazed in disbelief. Finally, he said, "Our mission went fine. What happened with Jason?"

"From what I was told, we used the bridge and tunnel strategy one time too many. All the bridges and tunnels were being guarded by hidden Freedom Troopers."

"No wonder there were hardly any guards at the Treatment Center last night," Patrick said. While Patrick felt a twinge of guilt for coming up with his own plan, not following Jimmy's advice had probably saved the lives of Patrick and his rebel band.

"As if you haven't screwed things up badly enough, Jason's death leaves us with another problem," Jimmy said, "Megan already knows, of course. She suspected the worst last night when Jason didn't come home. I gave her the news first thing this morning. Megan needs to disappear – and fast."

"What do you mean?" Patrick asked.

"It won't take long until the government links Jason to Megan. They're already posting photos of all four men who were killed and offering a reward for any information about them. If Megan gets picked up for questioning, she'll almost certainly crack and give us all up. Nothing against her, she's as strong as anyone we know, but eventually they'll make her talk."

"So what's the plan then?"

"We have to help her disappear. Our friend Mr. Johnson has already deleted her employee records. I need to stay out of sight as much as I can. So I'm going to stay here and stand watch. I want you and Kristina to go pick Megan up, pack as much of her personal shit in your car as you can, and make sure you take all the weapons Jason had stashed at the house. Then drive Megan anywhere she wants to go, but it has to be far away. A hundred miles absolute minimum; further would be better."

"How will she live, for Christ sake? What do you want me to do, Jimmy? Dump her in the middle of nowhere and drive away?"

"Mr. Johnson gave me a good amount of cash for her. She'll be able to get started again somewhere, but it has to be far away from where she lives now."

"Kristina and I will go over and get her right now."

"The sooner you get her away from there the better. With the Independence Day celebrations going on all over the place, the Freedom Troopers will have their hands full today. That will help all of us. But try to stay on the back roads. Get going."

A few minutes later Kristina arrived in Patrick's car, weeping quietly, and they drove in silence to Megan's house. As they drove up to the modest house, Patrick and

Kristina saw that all the shades were closed. They found Megan sitting in a dark living room crying. At least she had thrown some of her personal belongings into a couple of cardboard boxes.

"I'm going to take a look around, Megan," Kristina said, "and make sure you packed everything you'll need." Within five minutes, Kristina returned to the living room with another box of Megan's things.

"All right," Patrick said gently, "we've got to get going." Each of the three picked up a box and took it to Patrick's small car. Megan paused for a couple of seconds and looked back into the house before she walked out.

"Where would you like us to take you?" Kristina asked.

"I...don't know," Megan answered. "All my family lives in this sector. I know I have some distant family in other places, but Jimmy said I can't even ask my mom who they are. He said no one can know I'm leaving." Megan began sobbing loudly.

"Here's what we'll do," Patrick said, "We're going to drive a hundred miles or so. Then we'll find you a place to squat. You'll be all right, Megan. I know you'll make it."

The long drive was made in almost complete silence. Three sectors away, Patrick and Kristina found an abandoned home that looked pretty good. It had a large yard and other people living nearby, so hopefully Megan would have a support network of some kind. They drove to a nearby store and bought food, water and other supplies. Patrick left one of the rifles and some ammunition that he had taken from Jason's stockpile.

"We'll come back in a few days," Patrick assured Megan, "and get some kind of electrical generator set up for you. Are you going to be OK?"

Megan nodded tearfully, and Patrick could tell by the look in her eyes that she would do what it took to survive. As he and Kristina drove away in the early evening, Patrick couldn't help but think that Jason and Megan had paid the ultimate price to fight for freedom on this Independence Day.

Entry Twenty-Two:

Independence Day, July 2025

Steve and his family were enjoying the Independence Day celebration, even though the Freedom Troopers were present in large numbers. There were a few scuffles between the Freedom Troopers and groups of protestors, and Steve was happy that he had chosen to blend in with the crowd on this day rather than join the protests as he had in previous years. He made a point of wearing a baseball cap and kept it pulled low to try to avoid having his face scanned by the many cameras mounted on poles in the town square.

The fireworks were scheduled to begin shortly after nightfall, which would cap off the day of celebration. The park was even more crowded than it was earlier in the day.

As dusk came, another clash broke out. A group of protestors who had been noisy but peaceful throughout the day suddenly became agitated. One of the members of their group had leaned over a retaining fence into an off-limits area and was struck in the side of the head by a Freedom Trooper's rifle butt.

As the protestors looked at their comrade's profusely bleeding head, their anger mounted. Several of them started throwing various objects at the nearby Freedom Troopers.

"There's going to be trouble over there," Steve said to his wife as he pointed at the protestors. "Maybe we should move away from them a little."

"Oh, you worry too much," his wife answered, "this is a perfect spot to see the fireworks, so we should just stay here. Besides, there are too many people around us; we wouldn't be able to move even if we wanted to."

A minute or two later, Steve gasped in horror. At least fifty Freedom Troopers wearing insect-like gas masks were marching five abreast, heading right for the group of protestors. They carried their automatic rifles in combat-ready position and all of them had a large supply of gas grenades.

Steve realized that he and his family were squarely in the path between the marching Freedom Troopers and the protestors. He stood up and shouted, "We have to get out of here – now!" But by that time the crowd around them was also trying to get out of harm's way and the four of them were caught in a crush of people.

The scene quickly degraded into mass confusion and panic – fleeing people trampled those who reacted more slowly and were still sitting on the ground. The Freedom

Troopers continued marching toward the protestors, forcing their way through the crowd by swinging their rifle butts back and forth, hitting whoever was in their path, and stomping anyone on the ground.

Frustrated that the families gathered for the fireworks were not getting out of their way, the Freedom Troopers in the front of the column began lobbing gas grenades into the crowd. Packed against one another and unable to move, people could not flee the gas clouds and many collapsed. Those in the crowd who didn't succumb to the gas trampled on the unconscious bodies that were blocking their escape path.

In the meantime, the protestors were now throwing every object they had at the approaching Freedom Troopers, and in their panic they were hitting just as many innocent bystanders as soldiers. Screams filled the air from all directions.

As the column of Freedom Troopers moved closer, they broke ranks and surrounded the protestors on two sides.

When the Freedom Troopers were in place, the commanding officer shouted a few words and the soldiers raised their rifles. The commander shouted again and the sound of automatic gunfire filled the air, followed by an acrid haze of gunpowder smoke.

In a few short minutes, the city park went from being happy and festive to almost complete silence. The only sound was the whimpering of a few children and the anguished cries of wounded men and women. Forty protestors lay dead on the ground, and at least fifty innocent spectators were also down and motionless. Many of the dead non-protestors were trampled to death by the crowd and an equal number were killed by stray bullets from the Freedom Troopers.

Among the dead on the ground were Steve's wife and two children. Steve knelt over them and screamed curses at the Freedom Troopers. A nearby soldier looked over, calmly raised his rifle and shot Steve through the head.

Entry Twenty-Three: July 2025

Patrick drove toward Mr. Johnson's house in the Wealthy section of Center City, stopped in front of the gate and flashed his headlights three times. As usual, the gate opened and Patrick drove up the driveway and straight into the open garage. Once he was inside, the garage door closed behind him. Jimmy's car was already there.

Mr. Johnson, Jimmy and his fellow rebel Mike were sitting at the kitchen table waiting for Patrick to arrive. The three men stood and shook hands with him.

"Good to see you Patrick," said Mr. Johnson. "This has been a difficult few days we've all had."

"You're goddamned right," Patrick said. "One of my good friends and one of my best soldiers are dead. Megan is in exile and trying to survive all by herself. Instead of grieving, Kristina and I have a hundred escaped Treatment Center patients living in an abandoned retail store that we're babysitting around the clock."

Jimmy grimaced and said, "I know it hurts. But I never said this would be easy. Let's talk about why I wanted to meet. Nearly a hundred people were killed three days ago at the celebration. Years from now, history books will say that Independence Day of 2025 was the start of the Great Class War. This is a turning point. We have to start making serious plans."

Mr. Johnson said, "I'm going to help you with at least one of your problems, Patrick. My company has quite a few dormitories that were built for employees who worked in the mines. Over the past couple of years, we've closed down some of the mines, so there are quite a few empty buildings. I'll re-open one dormitory and there will be plenty of room for your escapees. That particular mine is closed down, so no one will know that they are there. I'll make sure they have plenty of food and supplies. It's pretty remote so you won't have to worry about any of them leaving."

"Thanks, Mr. Johnson," Patrick said, "There are a couple of patients who've established themselves as leaders. I'll put them in charge."

"On the negative side," Mr. Johnson said, "there is a new Regional Commander that took over on July first. His name is Victor Nefario and he is bad, bad news. He's behind your friend Jason getting killed and the Independence Day massacre. The guy he replaced was a complete moron, but Nefario is extremely capable and bloodthirsty. From what I've been told, he's been given permission by the Supreme Command to use as much violence as necessary to quell the rebellion."

"That was bound to happen," Jimmy said quickly. "As soon as we made any headway, I knew they'd bring in a butcher. But that doesn't change our plans. Like I said, this is a turning point. Thanks to the massacre, public sentiment has really started to shift toward us. Now is the time to start recruiting in a big way."

"Tell them about what we discussed," Mr. Johnson said.

"We need to be better organized," Jimmy said, "so we're going to be more formal. Patrick, you and Mike are now each in charge of half of the area we cover. That makes me the General of the operation. You each have a lot of ground to cover. You'll need to recruit heavily – you should have at least three sub-commanders reporting to you, and they should each have six guys leading twenty-man squads reporting to them. That means you'll need close to four hundred rebels each. We can provide arms for them, but just having weapons isn't enough any-more – this new commander isn't going to be a push-over."

Mike asked incredulously, "Are you out of your mind? How am I going to recruit four hundred men?"

"You don't need to recruit four hundred men by your-self," Jimmy answered patiently, "in fact, I don't even want the street-level soldiers to know who you are. You need to recruit your three sub-commanders and maybe the six men that report to them. They'll recruit the rest."

"I just bought two old abandoned warehouses," Mr. Johnson said, "one for each of you. They can be used for training facilities and to store your weapons. I can't afford to pay the street-level soldiers, but the two levels of men directly under you will be paid by my corporation."

Patrick's head was spinning. His image of himself until now was that of a true rebel, attacking wherever and whenever the urge struck him. Suddenly he felt like a middle manager in a corporation, with several men reporting to him and the lives of four hundred men depending on his battle planning.

After they plotted strategy Jimmy said, "We'll meet here at Mr. Johnson's house every other Saturday morning. This is it. We're officially at war."

Entry Twenty-Four: July 2025

Colonel Nefario sat in his office, sipping a whiskey and water with a satisfied smile. The past few days could not have gone better. He sent the infidels a clear message by figuring out their attack strategy so quickly. There had been no ambushes since then.

The Treatment Center attack was a blemish on his early success, he admitted to himself. But with his Troopers not distracted by other duties like they had been the past few days, they'd track down the escaped faggots in short order. A hundred mental patients shouldn't be too hard to find. He wished he could be the one to administer the punishment once they were captured. That would be fun, he thought, but unfortunately it was the doctors who would enjoy that pleasure.

Nefario thought fondly about the past killing he had been involved with. While the dopey liberals called them atrocities, Victor Nefario looked at killing as one of the most profound actions a man could take. Murder was the ultimate exercise of power over fellow men.

One moment, there was a human being that existed. There was a good chance that he or she was loved, and loved others in return. Perhaps he had a wife and children, or she had parents who loved her. He may have had a life of accomplishment, or she may have been destined to do great things in the future. But with one powerful move he – Victor Nefario – could erase them from existence. Their memory would grow faint in the minds and hearts of their loved ones who still lived. Their past accomplishments would be forgotten and their future destiny snuffed out like a candle. Killing was the ultimate power, the Colonel discovered long ago. Once he made that discovery, he lusted after killing like many men lust after sex or money or power.

The ringing of his phone startled Colonel Nefario from his daydream. "Who is it?" he asked.

"The Supreme Commander is calling for you," answered one of his assistants over the intercom.

Probably calling to give him a promotion, Nefario thought. "Good afternoon sir," he said cheerily into the phone.

"What the fuck are you doing out there?" the Supreme Commander screamed into the phone. "You've been there five days and there are already – what – a hundred dead bodies? The dead included innocent women and children, for Christ's sake!"

"Sir, may I remind you that my orders were to do whatever it took, no holds barred, to get rid of the rebels."

The Supreme Commander hissed, "Have you ended the rebellion? Answer that question for me, you idiot! Instead of damaging the rebellion, you've made martyrs out of the protestors and completely turned public opinion against us!"

"Of course the rebellion isn't over. It's been less than a week. But rest assured that the past few days have been the first step in putting an end to it."

"Then why is the Chairman of the Board on my ass? His intelligence experts say that the majority of the people in your region now support the rebellion. Even the Wealthy class is saying that this was too much violence!"

Nefario squirmed in his seat. This reaction was totally unexpected, and he resented being screamed at like he was an unruly child. "All right, sir. I will tone down the violence. But let me remind you, there is only one thing that these rebels understand and that is fear. Either they must fear us or they will assume that we fear them. Which would you rather have?"

"Do what you need to do, Victor. But keep it under control. Get the people back on our side. That's what I'm saying." Nefario heard a loud click, the only indication that the call had ended.

The Colonel stared at his desk, deep in thought. Those weak sisters in Washington would never see it his way, he concluded. There was no hope for this government. It was time to start implementing his plan – the one that he had laid the groundwork for over the past six months while sitting on his ass at a desk in the bowels of the Pentagon. Those moron politicians thought he would take the humiliation they dished out to him without fighting back. Well, they could not have been more wrong. Even by transferring him to this Godforsaken region, they had played right into his hands. If things worked according to his plan, within a few months it would be payback time.

PART TWO

The insurgency will rise
When the blood's been sacrificed
Don't be blinded by the lies
In your eyes

- Green Day, "Know Your Enemy,"
from the album 21st Century Breakdown

Entry Twenty-Five: September 2025

It was as unusually pleasant summer morning and Kristina talked Patrick into going for a rare outing to the shopping area of Center City. Patrick had a good-paying job with Mr. Johnson's company, so for the first time in their adult lives they had a little extra money. Patrick actually worked very little on the job and had dedicated almost all of his time since early July to recruiting and training a rebel group of nearly four hundred men and women.

"Isn't shopping fun?" Kristina teased Patrick as they strolled along the sidewalk.

"You've never had the opportunity to shop much," Patrick answered with a laugh, "but I have to say that spending money seems to come naturally to you."

"It's a nice day to be outside. I know you don't like to be out in public much so it's fun when I can drag you out of the house."

"I just think it's better if I my face doesn't become too familiar around town," Patrick said. "Hey, what's with these signs all over the place?"

They walked up to a large poster that was stapled to the wood siding on a storefront. The sign said:

You Have The
FREEDOM
TO AGREE
With Your
Government

"Someone mentioned to me that signs like this have popped up in the past few days," Kristina said, "that's one reason I wanted you to come downtown." They walked a little further and saw another poster:

If You SEE Something
Then SAY Something!
Help Your Government
Stop the Terrorists
And Earn Cash Rewards

"What's this all about?" Patrick asked.

"There's a new campaign the government has started," Kristina said, "to counteract the damage that was done to their image by the Independence Day massacre. The national election scheduled for late November is another move to get people on their side."

"I'm sure the election will be a sham, but it gives people the impression they have some say in the government. I get the feeling from talking to people that the propaganda is working, at least a little," Patrick said. "There is still some support for the rebellion, especially among the lower class. But offering rewards to people for turning us in was a smart move on their part. They're trying to turn the underclass against one another."

"How is the training of your recruits going, by the way?"

"Not bad. But with all the time we spend in training, we haven't been able to do many actual attacks. Since Independence Day my guys have done two ambushes and I think Mike has done the same. The attacks were all successful, but they were small potatoes; nothing like the armory or the Treatment Center."

"Some of the people I talk to say that the resistance seems to be losing momentum, that maybe the government has turned the tide," Kristina said.

"I know, and that bothers me. That's why we have to start taking action. But when we attack again, we need to do it right. Since that Nefario guy came in, things have been a lot more organized in the military."

"How close do you think you are to having your soldiers ready?"

"A week or two should do it," Patrick answered, "I'm meeting with Jimmy and Mike this week. We've got to do something to get the momentum back on our side."

At that moment Patrick heard a woman's voice say, "Hello Patrick!" He looked up to see Jenna Johnson, walking down the street with her arms full of shopping bags.

Patrick could feel his face turn red. "Hello, Jenna," was all he could muster. He could feel Kristina's discomfort, and he quickly added, "Jenna, I'd like you to meet my friend Kristina. This is Jenna Johnson, she's Mark Johnson's daughter. I've mentioned him to you."

Kristina smiled and nodded at Jenna, "Hello, it's a pleasure to meet you. A beautiful day, isn't it?"

After a minute more of uncomfortable small talk, Jenna found a reason to be somewhere else and continued down the street. Patrick and Kristina stood in uncomfortable silence.

"You've mentioned Mr. Johnson many times, but you never said he had a beautiful daughter about our age," Kristina said, "and apparently you two have become acquainted."

"It wasn't relevant," Patrick said weakly, "she's just his daughter; she doesn't really get involved with me."

"I'm a woman, Patrick. We have a sense for things like this, and I can tell you for a fact that this Jenna Johnson has a thing for you. And you aren't any better. You stood there acting like a nervous schoolboy."

Patrick kissed Kristina in a rare display of public affection. Patrick was very wary about showing affection outside of their home, since mixed race couples were frowned upon by the government. "You have nothing to worry about," Patrick said.

"Hmmm," Kristina answered.

Entry Twenty-Six: September 2025

Colonel Nefario leaned back and put his feet up on the desk. "It's been a long day. Sergeant Randall, will you mix us a couple of drinks?"

Rick Randall brought a whiskey and water to the Colonel and sat across the desk with a drink of his own. It looked like another long evening of getting half-drunk with his commanding officer, listening to him strategize and complain about the wimps in Washington. It was becoming a pattern for him to get home very late a couple of nights a week, and his wife was growing increasingly angry about these evening sessions. It was making his home life unpleasant.

Colonel Nefario had seen his power and influence grow over the past two months. After the initial reaction from the Independence Day incident settled down, the Colonel presented a plan to the eggheads in Washington and had finally gotten his point across to some important people.

One of the changes he suggested several months ago was already implemented, and that was the division of the continental United States into five military regions. Nefario was Regional Commander of the Near West Region, which included the area from what were previously Montana, Wyoming and Colorado on the west edge to Wisconsin and Illinois in the east. The Colonel kept his headquarters in Center City since that area seemed to be the current hotbed of rebel activity.

"What's the status of the supplies we need to start implementing the relocation program?" Nefario asked his assistant.

"We have a couple of thousand tents arriving by the end of next week."

"That's a good start, but we need to get those old FEMA trailers shipped out here as well. It's going to start getting too cold for tents in the northern part of the region," Nefario answered.

The Colonel had talked Washington into letting him test a new program in the Near West Region. His idea was to relocate the vast majority of the lower class into remotely located government housing settlements, where they would be removed from the urban areas and easier to control. What better way to manage the infidels and squash the rebellion than to isolate them far away from civilized society?

Of course, that wasn't the way his idea would be presented to the underclass – there would be plenty of carrots offered, and if that didn't work, then Nefario would bring out the stick. The Colonel's goal was an aggressive one – he wanted at least half the underclass in his region to be in relocation camps by the November election.

"Your idea to secure those old FEMA trailers is brilliant. The trailers were used by the Federal Emergency Management Administration to house people who were the victims of natural disasters like hurricanes. But most of them haven't been used in a decade," Rick Randall said.

"The real coup was getting Washington to give me a huge grant to pay the infidels to repair and update the trailers. Giving those underclass people jobs will attract them like flies to the government housing projects."

"It's a great plan. Free housing, a little bit of vacant land where they can farm, and a chance to earn some money to get started in their new homes. If this works, you may go down in history as one of the great leaders of modern time."

Nefario laughed and said, "Let's not get ahead of ourselves, Sergeant. First, we need to convince the underclass to relocate. We've softened them up a bit and should build some trust with our posters. I've hired a great PR firm to work on the relocation campaign. Getting those lazy bums to pack up and move will be a major sales job."

Within a few days, the relocation program was announced to the public. As Nefario predicted, the promise of jobs to people who had been unemployed almost all their lives attracted a great deal of interest. The first week alone, over five thousand families in the region registered for relocation. The first relocation camp was opened in a remote area about fifty miles from Center City.

Entry Twenty-Seven: September 2025

Jimmy was in a foul mood when Patrick sat down at the table in Mr. Johnson's kitchen.

"About fucking time you got here, Patrick. We are losing the war," Jimmy said, slapping the kitchen table to make his point and looking Mike and Patrick in the eyes. "We had everything going our way in July and they've turned things around on us. We have to get the momentum back. Are your guys ready for some action?"

"I think my guys are prepared," Mike said. "But I'm not sure of a strategy. What are our targets?"

Patrick was thinking the same thing. He had a small army trained, but what should they attack?

"First thing, we need to go back to our plan of hitting the Patriot Squad patrols. Remember, we have to strike fear into them. With our larger numbers and a good supply of weapons, we won't have to resort to guerilla attacks. We can meet them head-on and outfight them if we plan it right."

Mike said, "That should work, but we have to be smart. And we need the element of surprise. Patrick, between the two of us, we should be able to come up with twenty squads – right?"

"I have a few hundred men right now, and if you have the same number, then we can do it. If we time it right and attack a bunch of Patriot Squads all in the same night, it would put a huge dent in the government troops. That would be a major victory for us; just the big splash we're looking for, Jimmy."

"I like that idea. A big strike and then disappear for awhile. We don't want the government to be able to react and guess our next move. That's what led to the disaster in July," Jimmy answered. "The question is: can you guys swing this? There's a lot of planning and intelligence that need to happen."

Patrick said, "It will take about two weeks for me to get it set up. My area leaders can provide the intelligence; I've had them monitoring Patriot Squad movements for the past month so we know where we can find them."

"Same with my guys," Mike said. "We've been gathering information on patrol routes so it's just a matter of lining up the men and going over the mission details with them."

"Okay then," Jimmy said, "let's shoot for two weeks from today. We'll meet here two days prior to finalize every-thing. Mr. Johnson, do you have anything to add?"

Mr. Johnson looked worried and said, "Time is very much of the essence. The government just announced plans to start relocating the lower class. They're going to segregate the lower class miles away from the rest of society. They've already started rolling out the plan, and it's been very well received. At the rate things are going, within two weeks, you may start losing a lot of your men."

"Christ almighty!" Jimmy shouted. "That would put us out of business. Most of our fighters are from the underclass, and if we lose them, it could be the end for us. Mike and Patrick – how quickly can we get these attacks done?"

Mike and Patrick glanced at each other before they answered together, "One week, if we have to. We'll make it happen."

Entry Twenty-Eight: September 2025

Colonel Nefario packed his bags and hopped into the military vehicle next to Rick Randall. "We have a long drive to Colorado, so let's get on the road," Nefario said.

Part of the Colonel's responsibility as Regional Commander was to oversee the operation of the NORAD, the North American Aerospace Defense Command. This was the organization that was previously responsible for the air defense of the United States and Canada, including launching nuclear weapons at enemy countries.

With the decline of the rogue nuclear powers of North Korea, Iran and Pakistan, the door was opened in 2020 for the Great Nuclear Treaty, which called for the disarming of all nuclear missiles worldwide. Most NORAD facilities were shuttered following ratification of the treaty. However, untrusting as they were of one another, the governments who still retained nuclear capability kept their missile stockpiles fully intact; they simply switched off the mechanism that allowed the missiles to be fired.

The main missile control center in the U.S. was located near Colorado Springs in a building that was commonly

referred to as "Cheyenne Mountain." Nefario had responsibility for ensuring that the nuclear missiles in his region were safely stored, but the missiles also needed to
be kept at the ready so they could be re-armed on short
notice should other countries violate the treaty. The men
under Nefario's command operated the control center
that could launch missiles that were in secret locations
throughout the nation.

"Wow, this is an impressive place," Rick Randall said as
they drove through a pair of extremely heavy-looking
metal doors and entered a tunnel leading into the side of
the granite mountain.

We still have a quarter-mile to go before we get to the
actual command center," Nefario said, "once we're there,
we'll be surrounded by at least two thousand feet of
granite on all sides. There are actually fifteen separate
buildings in the mountain, they're connected via tunnels.
The shell of each building is made of three-eighths inch
steel."

"Wow, this is really something," Randall said.

Nefario continued his lecture, "Believe it or not, each
building is mounted on a set of springs to absorb the
shock of a nearby nuclear blast, and can move twelve
inches in any direction. Supposedly this place can with-
stand a nuclear bomb within a mile away. This is where
you want to be when...I mean if, the nukes start flying."

Sergeant Randall pulled the car into a parking spot and the two men walked into the main command building. They were greeted by a tall, heavy-set officer who looked almost as imposing as Victor Nefario.

"Colonel! Good to have you here," the officer said, saluting the senior officer.

"Great to be here, Captain Harris," Nefario said while returning the salute. "This is my top assistant, Sergeant Richard Randall. Rick, meet Captain Daniel Harris. He's the commander of the entire facility."

"Good to meet you," Daniel Harris said blankly to Rick Randall.

"Are you getting settled into your new home?" Nefario asked. "Is the family happy with the move to Colorado?"

"We love it here. The mountains are incredible," the Captain answered, "and my wife is happy with my promotion."

Nefario said, "Rick has never been here inside of Cheyenne Mountain. Can you arrange for someone to give him a tour for the next hour or so?"

"No problem," Harris answered, and made a quick phone call. Within a minute, two junior officers whisked Sergeant Randall away. Captain Harris closed the door and sat behind his desk.

"I'm here to personally check on your progress," the Colonel said. "As you know, some matters can only be discussed in person. So tell me where you're at in your preparations."

Captain Harris answered, "Every one of the fifty men and women working in this facility are completely loyal to me. It's a skeleton crew; in the old days there were at least two hundred people working here. But the fewer people involved, the better off we are."

"Good thinking," Nefario answered, "as long as the work gets done. What about arming the missiles?"

"I'm working on that," the Captain said confidently. "Of course, I can launch any missile in the country from here, but someone with a lot of expertise has to physically get into the missiles to arm them again. The ones located in the Near West are no problem at all. I have my own hand-picked team of experts working here and they are loyal to me. For other parts of the country, I've been able to infiltrate some of my men into the teams that maintain the missiles. But we're not going to get them all armed, Victor. It just isn't possible without someone taking notice."

"How many missiles can we get armed without raising suspicion?"

"I have men placed on two different teams. Each team covers a region, so we have three out of the five regions covered. The area is pretty much the entire West Coast and East Coast as well as the Near West."

Victor Nefario broke into a wide grin, "That's fantastic, Daniel. With your contacts and knowledge about the nukes, I knew you were the man for this job. And believe me, if we pull this off you'll be richly rewarded."

"If we *don't* pull this off, we're going to be hung or face a firing squad," Harris answered.

Nefario laughed and answered, "So we damn well better do it right. Let me know when you've armed all the missiles that we can get to. So, your family likes it here, huh?"

The two men engaged in small talk until Sergeant Randall returned from his tour. Nefario stood up and shook the Captain's hand, "Daniel, you seem to have everything under control here so we're going to get out of your hair. We have two stops to make on the way back; I want to pop in on a couple of people."

Rick Randall had plenty of windshield time to dwell bitterly on the situation in which he found himself. Nefario had promised him the next big promotion in the region. He put in five long years with the asshole, working eighty hours a week and putting up with his bullshit. And what happened? A great assignment opens up and Nefario brings someone in from outside his personal staff.

Plus, Randall was sure that something strange was going on with the Colonel. He was certain that Nefario was holding back information and not telling him what his true plans were. All he could do at this point was play along and pretend that all was well. But when the time came, Rick Randall decided at that moment he would do whatever it took to survive in his career. He would not go down in flames with that lunatic.

Entry Twenty-Nine: September 2025

Patrick stood in front of his sub-commanders, all of whom were looking at him like he was a god of some sort. They had done a great job recruiting and training their units, but they still had not faced serious combat. Tonight, Patrick was laying out the details of the plan to attack, and hopefully wipe out, ten Patriot Squads all in one night.

"You'll have forty men in your units," Patrick said to his men. He handed each of them a packet containing a map and precise layout of the surrounding area. "We've scouted these areas carefully and they present the best chance to surprise the enemy from higher ground. It's important that you stick exactly to the locations on these maps and place your men where I've indicated – I've put a lot of planning into this and freelancing is liable to get you and your men killed."

"Where will you be during the attacks?" one of the men asked.

"I'll choose one unit and tag along," Patrick answered, "I'm just as anxious as you guys are to see some action.

We'll meet here tomorrow night. I have some transportation lined up to take your guys where they need to be.
Make sure your men dress in dark colors, and above all
make sure they keep their mouths shut between now and
tomorrow night. The last thing we need is to have the
government hear that we're planning attacks. OK, that's
it – see you tomorrow night. Study those packets."

About a hundred miles away, Mike was having the same
discussion with his men. Both Patrick and Mike had
spent countless hours with Jimmy over the previous
week, reviewing the routes of the Patriot Squads and
carefully mapping their battle plans. Unlike their previous attacks, the rebels would be well-briefed and completely prepared. Jimmy was determined to avoid major
losses in the rebel ranks.

The goal was to wipe out a large number of Patriot
Squads in one night. If successful, the rebels would eliminate several hundred of the enemy as well as seize their
weapons. Since the Patriot Squads were low paid part-
timers, Jimmy hoped that inflicting large casualties
would frighten the surviving soldiers into quitting. Of
course, there were still the Freedom Troopers to worry
about even if the plan worked. They were professional
and well-armed, but there simply weren't enough of
them to control a widespread rebellion without the help
of Patriot Squads.

***

Patrick reviewed the gathered rebels as they prepared for the critical battle. They were all dressed in dark clothes and looked ready for a fight. For most of them, this was the moment they had looked forward to for months. Patrick joined the group that had Kristina as one of the rebel soldiers.

About one in five of the rebel volunteers were women. At Kristina's insistence, Patrick allowed women to join the fight. Mike's rebel forces also had a large number of women fighters, since Kristina had encouraged Mike's partner Maria to convince him to recruit women.

As the rebels waited in the warehouse, ten box-shaped cargo trucks pulled into overhead doors. All the trucks were painted with corporate logos on the sides to look like delivery vehicles. The rebels piled into the cargo areas and the trucks drove each group to their destination.

Patrick carried a walkie-talkie that allowed him to communicate with his sub-commanders. It was absolutely crucial that the attacks start within moments of each other so the Patriot Squads could not warn others. Even though they had superior numbers, the element of surprise was important if the rebel attacks were to succeed.

The truck dropped them off and drove away to a secluded area to await the signal to pick up the rebels after the attack. About half of Patrick's rebel squad hid in a wooded area just off the street and the other twenty rebels were further down the road. The plan was for the first group to allow the Patriots to pass by them, and then come out of the woods to attack from the rear just as the second group surprised the Patriots from the front.

The ambush started out exactly as the rebels hoped – the Patriot Squad was completely taken by surprise and put up minimal resistance. Patrick was shocked at the savageness of his troops – these members of the lower class who had been beaten down for the past decade finally had a chance to exact revenge and they took full advantage. The battle was brief but very violent. The Patriot Squad soldiers were outnumbered and still short on weapons because of the earlier success of the rebels in cleaning out the local armory.

As the last Patriot soldier fell, Patrick heard a quiet buzzing sound coming from a distance. He looked up to see a plane flying within a hundred feet of the ground and heading right for the rebels.

"Head for the woods!" Patrick yelled as he ran as fast toward cover. He turned to see the plane swoop in on the remaining rebels who were still in the street. The plane began shooting, the rounds missing the rebels but ricocheting off the pavement.

"Go deep into the trees!" Patrick ordered. After a few moments of silence passed, he said to the squad leader, "get a head count and make sure everyone is here."

Within two minutes the squad leader came back,

"They're all here, Patrick. Two men were wounded, they were hit by bullet fragments that bounced off the pavement. They're all right, not much more than a scratch on them."

Suddenly, Patrick heard the buzzing sound again. "Everyone take cover!" he said. Patrick slid on a pair of night-vision goggles and ran to the edge of the woods. He saw the small plane heading right at him, but still a hundred yards away. He raised his automatic rifle and sprayed the air around the plane with bullets. He must have hit something important, because the plane began smoking and flying erratically.

An instant later, a missile whizzed fifty feet above their heads, fortunately missing the rebels by a good distance. The explosion was deafening but far enough away that no one was injured. The small plane flew off into the distance, billowing smoke.

Patrick said to the squad leader, "Get that truck to pick us up right now. We need to get out of here, and fast. But tell the driver not to stop if he sees any small planes in the vicinity."

The sky was clear of planes three minutes later when the same truck that dropped them off stopped on the road near the woods. The rebels quickly jumped into the cargo area and headed back to their warehouse headquarters.

"What was that thing?" Patrick asked Kristina.

"I don't know for sure, but doesn't the government have drone planes? You know, small planes that are unmanned and flown by remote control?"

"That had to be what it was," Patrick said. "It didn't look big enough to hold a pilot. But I thought the government had a policy against using drones against their own citizens. Damn! I wanted us to get the weapons off those soldiers. That's thirty guns and lots of ammo we could have used."

Entry Thirty: September 2025

The next morning, Mr. Johnson and Jimmy greeted Patrick and Mike with a hearty handshake, "That was a great effort!" Mr. Johnson said, "My sources say you wiped out about one-third of the Patriot Squads in your sectors in one night. You can bet that the Regional Commander is wondering what hit them."

Patrick answered, "It went perfectly for Mike's guys. And it went well for most of my team, too. The only group that had trouble was the one I happened to be with. And we made it out with no casualties."

Jimmy interjected, "Mark, tell them what you've heard."

"There was a delivery made earlier this week, four flatbed trucks. The government has brought in ten drones. Some are spy planes only, but the others are armed with missiles."

Patrick said, "You don't have to tell me they're armed with missiles. I saw it for myself."

"These planes are very sophisticated," Mr. Johnson explained, "they all have night vision and infrared detection systems. The attack planes shoot pretty good sized missiles. These aren't like regular manned planes. They're smaller than a manned plane and they're very quiet. You won't know they're coming until they're right on top of you."

"No kidding," Patrick said, "All we heard was a buzzing sound when it got within a hundred yards or so."

"You're lucky that you disabled that plane, Patrick," Jimmy said, "from what Mark was telling me they aren't that easy to shoot down."

"How are we ever going to compete with those?" Mike lamented.

"We still don't know where they take off and land from," Jimmy answered. "Until we know that, we can't do anything but be ready to deal with them."

"It could be from anywhere," Mark Johnson said. "They can control them from hundreds of miles away, even further."

"Do you have any plans for our next targets?" Patrick asked.

"No attacks for the next week or two. I'm going to try to find out where those drones are flying from," Jimmy said. "But I have a project I want you two to work on. We need to have a look at the relocation towns that are springing up all over. I'm convinced there is something sinister behind them, but people are flocking to these trailer and tent cities – they're swallowing the government's promises like a hungry fish swallows a worm on a hook."

Mike said, "Have you stopped to think that maybe the government is really trying to help the lower class, Jimmy?"

"Not a chance," Jimmy spat, "I'll never believe that."

"Regardless of what their intentions are," Mr. Johnson said, "there are now twenty thousand people signed up for relocation. Hundreds of trailers are arriving every day."

"Patrick and Mike," Jimmy asked, "is there any way you can get into one of the relocation cities without drawing too much attention to yourself?"

"It shouldn't be too hard," Mr. Johnson said, "there are so many construction workers around the relocation cities that it should be a simple matter to blend in. Just wear work clothes and pick up a hard hat from my office."

Entry Thirty-One: October 2025

The largest of the new trailer cities was about fifty miles from Center City, so Patrick decided to visit there. Wearing a hard hat, flannel shirt and blue jeans, he was certain he would look like a hundred other workers.

Even though he knew what to expect from Mr. Johnson's description, the sight of the trailer city as he approached from a distance took Patrick's breath away. The perfectly aligned rows of shining white trailers stretched over the rolling hillside as far as the eye could see. In between the rows of trailers were narrow gravel roadways, about ten feet wide. Heavily insulated water and sewer pipe ran along the edge of the narrow roadways, and hastily strung electrical lines ran overhead.

Behind every trailer was a small garden plot, about ten feet wide and the length of each trailer. Patrick assumed that these were the "mini-farms" that the government touted in the brochures they were handing out to the lower class. According to the brochure, every family that relocated would be guaranteed a year's employment for at least one household member, a cash stipend, free education for the children and a mini-farm.

Patrick thought to himself that the reality didn't quite match the glamorous, flowery description in the full-color government brochure he had read. The trailer city seemed stark and impersonal, very much like a government housing project. Every trailer looked exactly the same and Patrick wondered how people could find their own home among a sea of hundreds of exact duplicates.

There were six large buildings that looked like they were simple metal structures. One appeared to be a school and one was an administrative building of some kind. Both had flagpoles in front of them. A third building, the largest, looked like a general store that had signs advertising groceries and supplies. It wasn't apparent what the functions of the other buildings were.

Dust filled the air as new trailers were towed into the city over the gravel roads. Children played in dirt and mud, and families sat on the small wooden steps that led to each trailer's one and only door.

Patrick stopped to talk to one family who was sitting on their steps. "Hello!" he said enthusiastically, "I'm hoping you can help me. My family is thinking of relocating here. Can you tell me about your experience and whether you're happy you came here?"

Before the man could answer, the woman on the steps said happily, "We love it here! Ted has steady work for the first time in years and we've got plenty of food."

"How do you like the trailer you live in?"

"It's a crap hole," the man said.

"It is not!" his wife argued, "it *is* a bit small for us and the two kids. But it's clean and it came fully furnished. Plus it has a nice heater, and the government pays for the electricity. Our kids are going to school for the first time ever!"

"What are we going to do when my job runs out in a year?" Ted asked his wife. "Where will the money come from then? We got suckered into a bad deal, that's what I think. There's nothing to do here but work my ass off or sit on these steps and stare off into space."

"Do you mind if I look inside?" Patrick asked.

The trailer was small, about fifteen by forty feet in size. Even compared to the small home he and Kristina once shared with four other people, the trailer looked extremely cramped. It was hard to picture two people living happily in there, let alone a family of four.

"It really is a nice place," the wife said, shooting her husband a look that clearly told him to keep quiet.

"Seems all right," Patrick said, "but how much does the government intrude in your life when you live here?"

"That part of it isn't too bad," the wife said, "If Ted misses work or the kids skip school, we sometimes get a visit from a Freedom Trooper. And if you break any of the rules, you get thrown into jail in a heartbeat. You would think they'd kick some of the troublemakers out of the city, but they seem to want everyone to stay."

"Yeah," the husband said, "there are some real bad apples living around here. The government doesn't seem to make any effort to screen out the criminals. And when they do act up, instead of kicking them out of the city, they're tossed in jail for a week or so, which doesn't get rid of the problem. The people who *want* to leave are told that they signed a contract and that they must live here for at least a year. I suppose that's how they keep their cheap labor from running out on them."

"Huh," Patrick said as he thought about that statement. "Well, thanks for the information. I'll give it serious thought."

"If it were me, I'd stay where you are," the man called out as Patrick walked away.

Patrick was investigating the larger buildings in the common area when he saw a military vehicle speed up the gravel road. After the vehicle stopped, a large, imposing figure in a dress military uniform hopped nimbly out of the passenger seat and walked toward the entrance to one of the large buildings. Patrick had guessed earlier that the building was some sort of government administrative facility.

Deciding to have some fun on the spur of the moment, Patrick hurried toward the entrance.

As Colonel Nefario neared the entrance, Patrick made a point of cutting him off and walking very lazily so that the Colonel would have to slow his urgent, fast-paced stride.

"Pardon us!" Sergeant Rick Randall said rudely to Patrick. Patrick ignored him and slowed down even more, placing himself in a position where the two officers would not be able to pass by.

"Jesus Christ, son," Nefario said as he gritted his teeth. "Some of us have things we want to get done today! You'll never be a success in this world if you walk around like a fucking turtle."

Patrick stopped directly in front of the entrance door, blocking their way. His eyes were about the same level as the Colonel's medal-laden chest, and Patrick saw the huge officer's nametag said *Colonel Victor Nefario*. "Excuse me, sirs," he said, putting the dumbest expression on his face that he could muster, "but I want to apply to live here. My cousin, he lives here and they gave him a good job and lots of money! Do you think they will let a three-time convicted felon live here? I haven't been arrested in over six months."

Nefario couldn't stand it anymore and swung his massive arm like a hook at Patrick, who was swept out of the doorway and completely off the sidewalk. Sergeant Randall quickly opened the door to allow the Colonel to enter.

Patrick walked away with a grin at having been a pebble in the shoe of the mighty Regional Commander. As he walked, he saw a large poster on the front of the building he now realized was the security station and jail. It said:

RELOCATION:
YOUR GOVERNMENT
MAKING YOUR
LIFE BETTER

His smile faded as he thought of the propaganda battle the rebels seemed to be losing. Suddenly his arm ached painfully where Nefario had hit him.

Entry Thirty-Two: October 2025

Nefario sat down across the desk from John Taylor, the Chief of Security for the relocation city. He was still irritated by his encounter with Patrick. "What is it that's so important I have to come out to this shithole to talk to you?"

"I've got a real problem, Colonel, and I wanted you to see it in person," John Taylor said seriously, "this relocation city currently has less than one-half the population you are projecting, and already our jail is overflowing."

"Then expand the jail. It's a fucking prefabricated metal building, for Christ's sake. I'll appropriate some funding for you to double the size."

"Expanding the jail is just putting a bandage on the problem. The fact is there are too many criminals that have relocated here, really bad people. And you won't let me kick them out of the city, which is what we should do."

Nefario pointed his finger at John Taylor and said menacingly, "Don't you dare tell me how to do my job. You don't get the big picture of what's going on. Just keep things under control and follow orders. If you have too many prisoners, make the jail larger. It's as simple as that."

"With all due respect, sir, I don't think you understand the seriousness of the situation. There are murderers, rapists, child molesters living here...you name it, and we've got them. We're trying our best to maintain some semblance of order but it's a losing battle."

"Get this straight! I don't want those criminals back in the city where they can prey on the Employed and Wealthy. I want them here where the only people they can harm are their own kind."

John Taylor's face suddenly changed. In a flash, he understood the true purpose of the relocation cities. They were not designed to help the lower class gain better lives – they were giant prison camps intended to segregate the underclass from the rest of society.

Nefario read Taylor's body language and saw he had made his point. His tone was more conciliatory as he said, "Here's what we'll do. We'll double the size of your police force with top-notch Freedom Troopers. They will be ordered to show no compassion to criminals. The Freedom Troopers will perform some public executions; we'll make an example out of a few unlucky hooligans. At the same time, we'll expand the jail. You should be able to do that within a few weeks with all these lowlifes around here that we're paying to keep busy."

"I appreciate that, Colonel," John Taylor said formally, "I believe those measures will go a long way toward solving the problem."

"Good! I'm glad we were able to talk this through," Nefario said with a broad smile as he stood up and extended his hand, "you're doing a bang-up job here, Taylor. Keep up the good work."

"Thank you," John Taylor said meekly as he shook hands.

As they returned to Center City, Nefario said to Rick Randall, "Take care of the details on this. Reassign some Freedom Troopers to this trailer city. Try to find single guys who won't mind living there – give them free housing plus a nice bonus. I want the best Troopers out there, men who won't take any shit from those jailbirds. And while you're at it, contact the security chiefs at all the relocation cities. If we need to do the same thing in all of them, we'll do it. It's very important that the relocation facilities work, at least until the November elections."

Entry Thirty-Three: October 2025

Jimmy and Patrick crouched in the tall grass at the edge of the drone landing strip. Between them and the concrete strip was a ten-foot metal fence topped with curled razor wire and fifty yards of slimy marsh. Both men held rocket launchers they had taken from the armory raid. Kristina crouched behind them, leaning on a heavy ammo bag with extra rockets. She also had three automatic rifles and a machine gun mounted on a tripod.

"Mr. Johnson said this is the one and only runway used by the drones in this area," Jimmy said. "That small building is the control center. Supposedly there are a few soldiers in there controlling the drones. Mark said they aren't called drones; they call them *Unmanned Aerial Systems,* or UAS for short. Whatever they want to call them, since the planes arrived a few weeks ago, they've been sending them up every night for routine reconnaissance missions around the entire region. Actually, their range is much further. From that little shack, they could fly these planes around the whole country if they wanted to."

"What time do they usually take off?" Patrick asked.

"They should be taking off anytime now. They generally send them up one after another and bring them back in the same way. Mark Johnson was one of the many VIPs they invited in last week to see the planes in action."

"Won't this tip off the government that there's a leak among the VIPs?" Kristina said.

"I doubt it," Jimmy answered, "the government has to figure we would be looking for this place, so we could have gotten the location from any number of sources."

Suddenly a buzzing sound filled the air. The planes were lining up on the runway.

"OK, here we go!" Jimmy said, "Patrick, try to get two of them. These are heat-seeking rockets so let the plane pass overhead and then fire at its tail. Kristina, we'll take care of the first two planes so you wait for the third plane. Then spray bullets at a spot just above the runway as it's taking off. This needs to happen fast – the second you're done shooting, we pack up our stuff and run for the truck."

The drones were spaced one behind the other on the runway. As the first one went airborne, Jimmy waited patiently and after about ten seconds he fired at the tail of the plane. A few seconds later an explosion lit the sky.

By that time the second plane had just left the runway, and Patrick fired at the tail just as Jimmy had done, resulting in another explosion. Suddenly, a loud, piercing siren filled the air.

"Uh oh," Jimmy said, "we've been spotted. There will be Freedom Troopers here in a couple of minutes. You two pack it up and go. I'm going to take a shot at the control building."

Patrick watched Jimmy aim as he and Kristina hurriedly packed the weapons in their cases. The rocket left Jimmy's launcher and flew toward the small cinderblock building. It hit right below the roof and the entire structure exploded.

"Come on, Jimmy!" Patrick said, and helped pack his weapon. The three ran about a hundred yards through the tall grass to the waiting truck that they had concealed a little off the road.

Patrick jumped behind the wheel, with Jimmy and Kristina in the front seat with him. He kept the headlights off and drove as fast as he safely could down the pitch-black rural road.

"We got a couple of them anyway," Patrick said.

"Patrick...there's something wrong with Jimmy," Kristina whispered. Jimmy had turned as pale as chalk and was perspiring heavily.

"Jimmy, what's wrong?" Patrick said as he stared at Jimmy. The truck swerved dangerously close to a deep ditch.

"You watch the road, Patrick," Kristina said, "I'll look after him. Jimmy, what's the matter?"

"I can't catch my breath," Jimmy whispered, "pain in my chest, a lot of pain."

"Damn! I think he's having a heart attack!" Patrick said, "What should we do?"

"I'll get these military clothes off of him," Kristina said, "then you drop us off at the charity hospital. They don't ask questions there. I'll say he's my uncle."

"Yeah, they don't ask questions there and it's also a filthy dump," Patrick said. "But if we take him anywhere else they'll insist on seeing a government ID."

***

The next morning, Patrick drove to the charity hospital and asked to see Jimmy. Kristina had spent the night in his room, sleeping in a chair.

"You look a lot better than you did last night," Patrick said to Jimmy.

"I'm just really tired. They gave me some kind of drug, I don't know what. The doctor said it was definitely a heart attack. They did some tests and the doc says my heart has about had it."

Kristina wept quietly in the corner. She also talked to the doctor and the report was grim. Jimmy's heart was still generally strong, but he had major problems with one of the critical valves. At some point the valve would fail – the doctor said it might only last a few months, a year at most. In the meantime, Jimmy could function fairly normally, as long as he didn't exert himself.

"I'll be out of this crap hole in a day or so," Jimmy said with false enthusiasm, "and we'll have a meeting to plan our next move."

"All right, Jimmy," Patrick said as he patted him on the shoulder, "we'll get going now. I'll stop in tomorrow morning and we'll see if we can get you out of here."

"Don't forget about me!" Jimmy called out to Patrick as he walked away. "This place stinks. Get me out of here tomorrow."

***

Colonel Nefario slammed his desk so hard that the entire office shook. "Do you know how much those fucking UAS planes cost?" he screamed at Rick Randall, "those goddamned rebels took out millions of dollar's worth of hardware last night! Not to mention the control center! I had to pull a lot of strings to have those planes located here, and now they're useless to me."

"How did they find out where the landing strip was?" Sergeant Randall asked rhetorically.

"Not hard to figure. We didn't keep the location secret; in fact we gave public tours. We must have had a hundred people look at the place. It could be any one of those people or someone else, the contractor who laid the runway or anyone like that," Nefario said.

"You had the right strategy, Colonel. The idea was for the drones to strike fear into the rebels, not give them another target to attack. I'll give the rebels credit – they seem to know where to hit us where it does the most damage."

Nefario pondered the Sergeant's statement and started to gain control of his anger, "They've been a nuisance, but we'll strike back. We've spread ourselves pretty thin with these relocation projects, the PR campaign and all that stuff. But those things are the priority. We can put up with a little damage by the rebels for the short term. They'll eventually get what's coming to them."

Entry Thirty-Four: October 2025

Once Jimmy was out of the hospital, he was eager to hold another meeting with Patrick, Mike and Mr. Johnson.

Patrick arrived early, but Jimmy's car was already in the garage. He walked into the kitchen to find Jenna Johnson sitting at the table alone, eating a bowl of oatmeal.

"Good morning, Patrick!" Jenna said happily, "Jimmy and my dad are having a little pow-wow in the study. They'll be done in a while. Would you like some coffee or something to eat?"

"Coffee would be great," Patrick said as he sat down at the table.

As she put a steaming cup in front of Patrick, Jenna asked, "So who was that girl you were with when we ran into each other a few weeks ago?"

"That's Kristina, my partner," Patrick answered.

"You mean, like your girlfriend, right? Are you two serious? Partners for life, as they say?"

The expression "partners for life" was often used by the

lower class, because mixed race couples like Patrick and Kristina were not able to marry legally.

Jenna's pointed questions were starting to make Patrick unravel. "I don't know," Patrick said, "I suppose so, but I never really thought about it that way. It's hard to think about the distant future. Plans have a way of falling apart the way things are in the world."

"I guess I'm asking," Jenna said, looking directly into Patrick's eyes, "if you're interested in going out with me sometime."

Patrick felt his face getting red, a reaction only Jenna Johnson seemed to bring out in him. "Well, uh, I'm not sure about that. Like I said, I haven't given much thought lately to Kristina and our future."

Thankfully, Jimmy and Mark Johnson appeared through the doorway. Jimmy looked almost like his old self, maybe a little bit worn down. But his eyes had regained the determination and youthfulness that Patrick had seen many times before.

"Hey, Patrick," Jimmy said happily. "Good to see you. Is Mike here yet?" At that moment, Mike opened the door and walked into the kitchen.

"We're all here, so let's get started," Mark Johnson said.

"I'm feeling pretty good," Jimmy said, "but I can't participate in missions anymore. If something happened to me while I was out with you guys, I could end up jeopardizing the safety of anyone who was with me. So I'll be behind the scenes from now on."

"That's where you should have been anyway, Jimmy. You can't get away with trying to act like you're twenty-five," Mr. Johnson scolded. "Patrick, from now on you need to be in close contact with Jimmy and me. Over the next several months, you'll be assuming more responsibility for strategic planning."

Mark Johnson's point was not lost on anyone at the table – Patrick would be taking over Jimmy's role. Patrick just hoped it was later, rather than sooner.

"Mark and I discussed what happened with the drones," Jimmy said, "the UAS program has been shut down for the next month. They need to bring in new control equipment and that will take some time. There's a rumor that they may just control them remotely from Washington, but Nefario is fighting that."

"Now the question is, what's next?" Mike said.

"That's a very good question," Mark answered, "and exactly what Jimmy and I were discussing. I think we need to start guerilla attacks in the relocation cities. You know, blow up the common buildings, cut electrical lines, plug up the sewer system, things like that."

"I disagree with Mark on this," Jimmy said. "If we go after the relocation cities, we're attacking our own people."

Patrick thought for a moment. "Why do our activities in the relocation cities have to be violent or destructive? I agree with Jimmy, that hurts our own people. And with the popularity of the relocation cities, we've lost the support of the public that we had right after Independence Day. Why don't we be more clever and fight in other ways? Here's what I mean," Patrick said as he grabbed a paper napkin and pulled out a pen.

"This is one of the government posters I saw in the trailer city," Patrick said while writing on the napkin. "Why don't we just go in at night and change the posters? Plant the seed of discontent with the residents. Some of those people think they've never had it so good but many others are unhappy with the situation and feel they're being forced to stay against their will."

Mark Johnson looked down at the napkin, which said:

YOU HAVE THE
FREEDOM TO AGREE
WITH YOUR
GOVERNMENT

Patrick scratched on the napkin and changed it to:

YOU HAVE THE
FREEDOM TO AGREE disagree
WITH YOUR
GOVERNMENT
Support the rebellion!

"You're likely to run into some Freedom Troopers, they're the ones policing the cities," Mark Johnson said. "You're not going to avoid violence no matter what."

"Absolutely right, Mark," Jimmy said, "but that's to be expected. The men will be ready for them."

"Most of the entrances are gated now. You need to get past security guards. The only times security is somewhat lax are when the shifts change and construction workers are coming and going," Mr. Johnson said.

"I think the thing to do is go in during the day, when there are all those construction workers moving in and out," Patrick said, "then lay low until after midnight, do our damage and hide again until morning. Then slip out as the workers start going in and out again."

"Christ, this is getting more complicated than just blowing shit up," Jimmy said with a laugh.

"What about *real* missions?" Mike asked, "I have four hundred guys who are looking for action."

"We can continue ambushing the Patriot Squads," Jimmy said. "As long as you plan the attacks very carefully. Those drone planes hopefully won't be bothering us for a while, and many of the Freedom Troopers have been transferred to the relocation centers, so there aren't many left in the cities. Coordinate the attacks between you and Patrick – do them all on one night like we did last time. That gives us the element of surprise."

"The Patriot Squads are losing men like crazy," Patrick said, "they were always just a bunch of clowns who wanted to play soldier. They never counted on having to fight and risk their lives."

"Exactly like we counted on," Jimmy said. "Those Patriot goons are motivated by looking like big shots in their fancy uniforms and making a little extra money. If you study the history of revolutions, what's happening with the Patriot Squads is true of every dictator's army. We're motivated by ideas: freedom, equality and justice. Those are things worth fighting for, and worth dying for. Those Patriot Squads have nothing worthwhile to fight for. That's why we're going to win."

"It's ironic that they throw around terms like *freedom* and *patriot* like they own them," Mr. Johnson said. "But you're really the ones that are fighting for those things. You guys are the real patriots."

"Don't leave yourself out of that category, Mark. We wouldn't be where we are today without your support," Jimmy said.

"Enough patting ourselves on the back," Mike said, "Patrick and I will plan to make one more big strike. If we do it right, it will hopefully be the end of Patriot Squads in this area. Mr. Johnson, do you hear anything about what's happening in other parts of the country?"

"This is the strongest area for the rebellion right now," Mr. Johnson answered, "but other parts of the country are learning about what's going on here and the rebellion in those areas is picking up steam. The rebels definitely have the government worried. That's why they've scheduled the elections in November. But they are also recruiting Freedom Troopers as fast as they can."

Jimmy yawned and said, "I'm a little tired, you guys. Let's get back to work."

During his drive home, Patrick's thoughts raced in a dozen different directions. Jimmy was definitely not up to leading the rebels, and Patrick would soon be having a lot more responsibility placed on his shoulders. Plus, he had this underground mission at the trailer cities to plan. Not to mention the Patriot Squad ambushes that Mike was anxious to do as soon as possible. As if those things weren't enough to think about, the conversation with Jenna kept creeping into his mind.

Patrick wasn't sure of his feelings about Kristina. He was being honest with Jenna when he said he hadn't given their relationship any thought lately. The past six months, he had focused almost completely on the rebellion rather than his personal life.

When they first were together, they were madly in love. But the rebellion had taken over their lives to the point where he often thought of her more as his fellow rebel and housemate rather than a lover. Jenna Johnson was exciting, young, beautiful and wealthy. But he and Kristina had been through so much together...Patrick clapped his hands on the steering wheel. Why in the world would he even entertain the possibility of leaving Kristina? He banished the thoughts – as Jenna said, he and Kristina were partners for life and he had many more important things to worry about.

***

When Patrick arrived home, he searched for Kristina and hugged and kissed her like he hadn't done for months.

"What's that all about?" she asked.

"I've been thinking about it," Patrick said, "and I don't think I've been a very good partner to you lately. I love you very much."

"Oh, my darling," Kristina said as she stroked his hair, "I love you too. I know we've not been very attentive to each other. But I'm proud of you, and I love you more than ever."

As they discussed the plans for the vandalism at the trailer cities, Patrick said, "I'd really like to get all the cities done at the same time so the government isn't able to react. But frankly, I don't think my squads are up for it. Their mindset is to kill people and blow things up. I'm not sure they have the subtleness that this mission calls for."

Kristina's face lit up as she said, "I have a great idea. What about those hundred people from the treatment center? The ones who are living in the dormitory? They've been there for over two months now, Patrick. They've been training every other day and are eager to help. You've got to find something for them to do."

"That's perfect, baby! I've been trying to come up with a project for them. Here's what we can do...dress them all in flannel shirts, jeans and hard hats. We can split them into teams of eight and easily cover all the trailer cities in one night. Can you help me out on this mission? I've got a lot on my plate right now. Talk to Mr. Johnson and see if he can get us the clothes and hard hats, and some construction trucks."

Entry Thirty-Five: October 2025

Colonel Nefario slammed the phone down on his desk. "Fuck it!" he bellowed, "Washington is doing nothing to help me."

"Why is that, sir?" asked Rick Randall tiredly. Nefario had been in a bad mood lately. He tried to soft peddle the impact of the UAS control center being blown up and the mass resignations of Patriot Squad soldiers, but Randall could see that the recent rebel victories were eating him up inside.

"I just asked for more Freedom Troopers to replace all the Patriot Squads we're losing. They told me that they're working on it but it will be at least another month before we see more Troopers in the region. My plan will work in the long run, but in the meantime those fucking rebels are making me look like a fool."

"Keep your focus on what's important," Randall suggested, "the relocation cities are progressing and we have about one-third of the underclass registered. It's going very well, sir. You should be happy."

Nefario sighed, "You're right, Rick. That reminds me, we need to make another visit to NORAD next week."

"That's great, looking forward to it," the Sergeant said with a false smile. *Yeah, right. I'm looking forward to ten hours each way in an uncomfortable military vehicle, listening to your bullshit and then being reminded you passed me over for a big assignment.*

"We'll leave on Monday morning, 05:00 hours."

Entry Thirty-Six: October 2025

"Good morning, Colonel Nefario," said Daniel Harris with a crisp salute. "Hello, Sergeant Randall," he added blandly.

"Rick," Nefario said, "the Captain and I need to have a private meeting. Why don't you make yourself comfortable in that vacant office down the hall for a half hour or so?"

Once the office door was closed, Nefario sat down. "Give me a progress report, Captain."

"All nuclear missiles west of the Mississippi River are now re-armed and under control of this facility. We've had some difficulty in other areas and as a result we have only about thirty percent of missiles armed in the Mid-Central and Northeast regions."

"Shit! What do you mean by difficulty?"

"As I told you, I was able to place some of my men on the missile maintenance crews in those areas, but unlike the situation in the Near West, I don't have the whole crew working for me. The plan called for my men to secretly arm the missiles during routine maintenance visits. They reported that other workers on their crews were becoming suspicious. I decided it was better to stop than to risk being discovered."

"Smart thinking," Nefario said after some thought, "It's disappointing, but we can live with it. We're close to our objective; now isn't the time to be greedy. We've got enough missiles at our disposal to accomplish our goal. You've done brilliantly, Daniel."

"Thank you, sir."

"You should be aware that I will be moving here to the NORAD facility effective the first of November. That doesn't affect your role as the head of the center. Since you're operating a skeleton staff, there's plenty of extra room in this mountain for a few more people. And I want to be where the action is."

"Will you be bringing your staff here with you?"

"I trust Rick Randall, but he knows very little about what we're doing. I think he'll be on board with the plan. I'm not so sure about my other assistants, so they will be staying where they are. I'll come up with attractive assignments for them and keep them back in Center City. They'll think I'm doing them a favor."

"Very good," Harris answered, "So I can expect you back here next week."

"That's right. That will give us enough time to do what we need to do before the election."

Entry Thirty-Seven: October 2025

Patrick hopped into the back of the truck, joining Kristina and nearly forty other soldiers. "Are we ready for this?" he asked everyone.

"Damn right, we are!" yelled one of the men.

"Remember the briefing you received. Strike fast and be on the lookout for drones. They supposedly are grounded, but our intelligence said they can be controlled from thousands of miles away. If you see a drone, take cover and shoot at it. Also remember, tonight will be different than the last attack. This is a sniper attack. We'll have a position on high ground and from there we'll send a rocket right into the middle of them. The ones that survive will scatter, and the snipers will pick them off as they run. Got it?"

Everyone nodded and mumbled in the affirmative.

At that same moment, nineteen other rebel squadrons were traveling toward their targets, all in trucks disguised as cargo vehicles.

"If we're as successful as the previous attack, this could be a fatal blow to Patriot Squads in the area," Patrick said, "so let's make this a good one."

As planned, the truck stopped for only a few moments on the dark roadside, waited as the men poured out, and drove off to a nearby secluded area. Although the neighborhood was well populated, the steep hill at the side of the street was carefully chosen by Patrick for the tall grass and the strategic advantage it offered to the rebels. The Patriot Squad soldiers would be sitting ducks for an ambush.

"Okay, quiet everybody! Wait for my signal to fire the rocket," the squad leader said. Just then, the government soldiers appeared a hundred yards down the road.

When the Patriot Squad was directly in front of them, the rebel squad leader raised his hand and dropped it. A rocket whizzed toward the center of the Patriots.

"Incoming!" one of the soldiers screamed, but it was much too late. The rocket exploded, killing almost all of the Patriot soldiers instantly. The remaining six soldiers scattered in all directions. With over thirty rifles shooting at them, the rocket blast survivors made it only a few steps before they were gunned down.

Within seconds, the truck arrived and the rebels hastily piled in. "Count your men before we pull out," Patrick reminded the squad leader.

"All present," the squad leader said as he pounded on the front wall of the cargo bay, a signal to the driver to start moving.

"Go, go, go!" Patrick yelled to the driver at the top of his lungs.

"That was too easy," Kristina said to Patrick.

"It went perfectly," Patrick said, "Let me get the other squad leaders on the walkie-talkie and see how things went for them."

After a few minutes on the walkie-talkie, Patrick learned that every ambush had gone just as smoothly. "Mike and I are meeting Jimmy at Mr. Johnson's house tomorrow afternoon," he said to Kristina, "why don't you come along?"

"Why? I'm not a leader of any kind," Kristina answered. Then she thought a few seconds. Maybe she'd bump into Jenna Johnson there. She had a few things she'd like to set straight with her. "But it might be interesting. I'd like to go," she said.

Entry Thirty-Eight: October 2025

Jimmy, Mike, Patrick and Mark Johnson sat at the now-familiar kitchen table.

"That was an excellent job last night!" Jimmy exclaimed.

"To be honest, the rocket launchers were overkill," Mike said, "those Patriot Squads didn't stand a chance."

"True, but we have the weapons, so why not use them?" Jimmy answered.

"We're not complaining. It was good not to have close combat and have things go exactly as planned for a change," Patrick said. "Have you heard any reaction from the government yet, Mr. Johnson?"

"Nothing yet, but my sources had told me that before the attack, the government was already down to about seven hundred Patriot soldiers over four sectors. There have been mass desertions. If you guys are correct, you wiped out over three hundred last night, which is nearly half their troops. I can't imagine that the ones who are left will stick around."

"It strikes me as strange though," Jimmy said, "that there wasn't any response from the government from our last attack a few weeks ago. They aren't reacting with any sort of urgency. What do you make of that, Mark?"

"The Regional Commander is preoccupied with the relocation cities. They're moving people into those trailers at an incredible rate. They figure the rebel problem will be solved because there will be no one remaining from the lower class who isn't in one of the relocation cities. Your rebels will be easy to find within a few months because there won't be anyone else left."

Jimmy frowned, "That is a huge problem. Patrick, how is your little vandalism project coming along?"

"I'm working on it," Patrick answered, "And it isn't a *little* project, Jimmy. It's going to be much harder than ambushing Patriot Squads. We've got clothing – construction worker type clothes and hard hats – for a hundred people. I've decided to use the Treatment Center escapees for this. It is the perfect project for them. We're training all day tomorrow, and I'm shooting for early next week for the mission."

"Can I come and watch the training?" Jimmy asked, "I've been sitting on my ass for the past couple of weeks and it's driving me crazy. I promise, I'll just watch."

"Sure," Patrick said, "I'll pick you up in the morning."

While the four men met in the kitchen, Kristina and Jenna

Johnson were having an uncomfortable conversation in the spacious living room.

"This house is incredible," Kristina said as she stared out the back window at the huge lawn and beautiful landscaping. Kristina had never seen a manicured suburban yard; she was accustomed to the overgrown backyard farms that most houses now had.

"Thank you," Jenna said stiffly, "we enjoy living here."

Kristina decided to forego any more small talk and get to the point. "I couldn't help but notice the way you looked at Patrick when we bumped into you. And the way Patrick acted like a goofy schoolboy in your presence."

"He is so cute that way," Jenna said, "he seems so innocent, yet so strong."

"Listen," Kristina said, "Patrick is with me. That's the way it is and the way it's going to remain. You need to back off."

"Hold on a minute," Jenna interrupted. "This isn't between you and me. It's for Patrick to decide. Frankly, I think he could be very successful in life given the right support. He's a natural leader and very smart."

"You are so naïve," Kristina responded. "You have no clue what Patrick has been through in his life. He would never be happy with someone like you."

"Oh, really! That's what you think?" Jenna said angrily.

"That's right. Let me tell you a story. It was Patrick's twelfth birthday, the summer of 2010. His parents had been doing pretty well up to the economic crash in 2008. Then his dad lost his job in December of 2008, right before Christmas. His mom worked part-time and got her hours cut back to practically nothing. They both looked for work, but couldn't find anything. His parents were nearly fifty years old and unemployed in a lousy economy. They tried like hell, especially his dad, but had no luck except for odd jobs. They lost their house and burned through their savings."

"I get it, he had a bad childhood," Jenna said.

"I was telling you about Patrick's birthday. He knew there wouldn't be much. What he looked forward to the most was his dad spending the day with him and just wishing him a happy birthday. But he didn't get that, Jenna. Instead he found his father had hung himself during the night from a rafter in their garage. He wasn't able to afford anything for Patrick's birthday and it pushed him over the edge."

"Oh my God!"

"I knew Patrick casually then, we were middle school friends. He changed that day. Before that, he was a happy kid. He had a wonderful sense of humor, always goofing around. After that he went into a dark depression. He barely spoke for two years. I finally was able to break through to him, but he didn't show any spark of life until he decided to join the rebellion."

Jenna started saying, "You know, people like you think I've had an easy life but…"

"Spare me your bullshit," Kristina said, cutting her off. "There isn't a person in this country who has a happy life. If you're poor, you have nothing. If you're in the Employed class, you live in fear every day that you'll lose your crappy job and end up in the gutter with the lower class. If you're in the Wealthy class, you resent the government trying to control your every thought and action. But trust me, you and Patrick are from two different worlds. I understand the world he comes from and you don't."

With that, Kristina got up and walked into the kitchen.

Entry Thirty-Nine: October 2025

"What have these people been doing in the middle of nowhere for the past couple of months?" Jimmy asked Patrick as they made the two-hour drive to the mining facility where the former treatment center patients were living.

"We set up a training program for them," Patrick explained, "my squad leaders have been taking turns coming out here. They've drilled twice a week and had numerous classroom sessions and field training exercises. But they're getting restless, obviously."

"What's today all about?"

"This is a dress rehearsal. We've split them into groups of eight. All of them will be dressed like construction workers and one of our trucks will drop them near the trailer cities. They should be able to blend in with the workers during the evening rush. Once they're in, they'll hide and take off their construction clothes. Underneath the flannel shirts and jeans they'll be dressed in all black. They will hit all the signs in the city throughout the night, and then put their construction clothes back on and slip out at dawn among the other construction workers."

"What about Freedom Troopers patrolling the trailer cities?"

"Our guys will all carry small arms hidden in a tool box. The plan is to hide in the shadows and avoid the Freedom Troopers. But if they have to fight, they will."

"Maybe you can bullshit those escapees, but don't piss in my ear and tell me it's raining. If any of them are caught by Freedom Troopers, they'll be in big trouble. Remember, those cities are enclosed by ten-foot steel fence topped with razor wire. If they get locked in, they're goners. This could very well be a suicide mission you're sending them on, just to deface some signs."

Patrick sighed. "Like I told you, this mission is much tougher than ambushes. But that's exactly why we have to do it. Once the government has all the people housed in relocation cities, they'll have complete control over them. We've got to get those residents to want to leave."

"I know," Jimmy answered, "I'm with you, I guess. We have to do something. And I don't want to destroy the resources of the people living there or harm any of them."

Patrick pulled his car into the parking lot, which was filled with the same dozen cargo trucks that were used in the Patriot Squad attacks. The treatment center escapees were lined up in rows of ten, all wearing their construction clothes and hard hats.

"Christ, it looks like a Village People reunion," Jimmy said with a laugh.

"What people?" Patrick said.

"Never mind, it was before your time."

Patrick walked to the front of the group and said, "Today is our final practice session before the mission. I want to remind you, this is a voluntary mission. Because of the danger involved, no one will fault you if you decide not to participate." Patrick mentally crossed his fingers. If too many of them backed out, it would ruin his plans.

To everyone's surprise, only one person spoke up. It was the man Patrick had assigned to be leader of the group. "We met and talked about it, and decided every one of us is going. Those assholes tortured us, practically killed some of us. We owe them and it's time to settle the score."

"Great!" Jimmy said. "But keep in mind this isn't going to be a shoot 'em up. Stealth is the key to getting in and out of there alive. Stay away from the Freedom Troopers, don't try to fight them."

"We understand that," the leader said, "and we'll follow orders."

"Good," Patrick said, "let's get to work then."

After a hard day of training, Jimmy and Patrick made the long drive back to Center City. "Do you think they can pull it off?" Patrick asked Jimmy.

"You know what? I think they can. You've done an excellent job with them. They'll need a little bit of luck but hopefully they'll all make it out in one piece."

Entry Forty: October 2025

"Is it really necessary for me to move to Colorado?" Rick Randall asked Colonel Nefario.

"Only if you value your career," Nefario answered brusquely. He honestly didn't care one way or the other if the Sergeant came to Colorado Springs. In fact, he seriously thought about leaving him behind. But after much consideration, he decided that he owed Randall the opportunity, in return for his loyalty over the past few difficult years.

"All right. I'll talk to my wife this evening. A little more advanced notice would have made things easier, sir. You're talking about moving next week."

"That's the way life is for a career military man – and his family," Nefario said flatly.

"Of course, sir, you're right," Randall said as he planned how he would break the news to his wife.

As the Sergeant walked to the front office, he was deep in thought. Something was definitely going on that he didn't understand. Nefario had put all his time and effort the past few months into the relocation centers. Now, just when that project was going full-steam, he decides to move to Colorado Springs. It didn't make sense.

As he walked into the front office, the other three assistants gathered around him.

"What did you get?" one asked Randall excitedly, "we all got assigned to be in charge of security in a relocation city!"

"I'm moving to Colorado with the Colonel, I guess," Randall answered unenthusiastically. "When do you three leave?"

"Tomorrow morning!" another one answered. "This is a terrific opportunity for us. What's your assignment in Colorado Springs?"

"Not decided yet," Rick Randall answered, putting an end to the discussion.

With the other assistants gone tomorrow, the Sergeant would have free access to all the files in the office. And he could eavesdrop while Nefario was on the phone. There was still a week before they were leaving for NORAD. Maybe he could solve the mystery of what was going on between now and then.

Rick Randall's desk intercom buzzed. "Come in, Sergeant," Nefario's voice said over the speaker.

"I'm pleased with the progress on moving people to the relocation cities," Nefario said, "but as I expected, the remainder of the parasites are going to be a tough sell. It's time to drop the carrot and pick up the stick. Set up a meeting tomorrow with all the Area Leaders of the Freedom Troopers in the region. Tell them to get their asses on a plane and get here."

***

Nefario started his meeting with the Freedom Trooper leaders by saying, "We are currently at just over half of the lower class living in the relocation cities. The trailers are there and waiting for another twenty-five percent. I want those trailers filled by mid-November."

"I don't understand, sir," one of the Troopers said, "how are we supposed to do that?"

"Christ, do I have to spell it out for you? Your men go up and down the street in areas where the lower class dirt bags still live. You kick down their fucking doors and beat them with your riot sticks. Then you pull out a relocation contract and make them sign it. If they refuse to sign, shoot a few of them. That will get the point across."

One of the leaders growled, "Not to be contrary sir, but we are desperately shorthanded. You're aware that the Patriot Squads have completely fallen apart. My Freedom Troopers are struggling to keep some semblance of order among the lower class. Crime is at an all-time high, and there's much more crime across classes. If I assign my troops to this, there will be absolutely no one assigned to law enforcement."

"And your point is...?" Nefario asked rudely. He let the question hang in the air.

After several seconds of uncomfortable silence, Nefario said, "Start tomorrow. I want the processing center to tell me that they are receiving one thousand signed applications per day. Are we clear on that?"

"Yes, sir," the Freedom Troopers mumbled.

Entry Forty-One: November 2025

It was a cold and rainy afternoon when Patrick and the rest of his eight-person squad jumped out of the back of the truck and onto the mud and gravel road leading into the trailer city.

"Everybody grab your tool box. You should have a pistol, some ammo, markers, spray paint, food and water in there," Patrick instructed his squad.

"Wow, this place is gigantic!" one of the men exclaimed to Patrick, "How many people live here? There are rows of trailers as far as you can see!"

"I heard there are close to twenty thousand living here," Patrick answered, "This is the largest of the relocation cities but they're all supposed to be this big by the end of the year. Here's the gate, everybody just shuffle in among the other workers."

As the rebels walked through the gate, they saw that government posters were on display at almost every corner of the makeshift streets. In the large common area, every building had several large posters affixed to it.

"You can see that we have our work cut out for us. Split up into the four pairs we decided on so we don't call attention to ourselves. It'll be dark in about an hour. Until then, try to look busy. Walk like you have a destination in mind. If someone asks you where you're going, tell them one of the residences has a plumbing problem you've been asked to look at and you're trying to find it."

"Could you review the plan for how we're getting out of here?" one of the men asked, "I don't want to get stuck in this place."

Patrick replied, "We meet at the entrance gate tomorrow morning at 07:00 hours. That's when the flood of workers comes in for the first shift and the third shift leaves. If you're not there, we'll assume the worst and leave you behind. So be on time."

As Patrick walked near the perimeter, he saw the extraordinary security measures that had been put in place. The chain link fence was ten feet high and topped with curly razor wire. A Freedom Trooper was stationed every hundred yards on the inside of the fence. There were towers scattered throughout the city, each manned by an armed Freedom Trooper. Patrick also noticed workers installing pole-mounted cameras.

"Those towers are new. They might be a problem. I was told that the cameras aren't operational yet, but they look close to being ready," Patrick said. "Be very careful. You don't have to deface every poster. If there is any question of being seen, don't expose yourself."

As he spoke, Patrick was thinking that all the security seemed geared more toward keeping people from leaving the city than protecting the interior. Most of the security measures were near the perimeter fence, and the majority of Freedom Troopers were guarding the fence rather than patrolling the streets.

"Okay, let's split up now," Patrick said, and the men dispersed in pairs.

"Where are we going to hide out tonight?" his partner asked. "We certainly will be caught if we're wandering the streets all night."

"Right after nightfall, we'll head for the newest section of the city," Patrick answered, "there should be plenty of empty trailers to choose from; I just hope they don't lock them. We'll hang out in an empty trailer until midnight or so, and then we'll get to work. When we're done, we'll hide out in the same empty trailer until morning."

***

Rick Randall drove in silence while Colonel Nefario stared out the window. It was bad enough that he had to move with just a week's notice, but Nefario insisted that the Sergeant drive him and his things to Colorado Springs. That meant that at this moment Rick Randall's wife was behind the wheel of a small moving van, probably cursing the day she married him.

To make matters worse, the snowy season was well underway in the mountains and it looked like they were heading into some flurries.

Nefario finally broke the silence. "Rick, I wanted to tell you about your new assignment, and a little bit more about my plans. I hope you're on board with everything I tell you, because at this point you don't have a choice."

"What is my assignment, sir?"

"I'm promoting you to head of security for all of the relocation cities. Your official title will be Commandant. I'll be spending all of my time at NORAD and won't be traveling. You're going to be visiting the relocation cities on a regular basis to make sure security is adequate. It's a good assignment and a promotion for you to Captain."

"Thank you," Rick Randall said, while wondering why in the hell he was moving his family out to Colorado when he could live anywhere in the entire region to do that job.

"It's important that you and I are on the same page about the relocation cities," Nefario continued, "I need you to understand what we're trying to accomplish."

"I assume that the goal is to provide a safe, humane and productive environment for the lower class citizens," Randall said.

"True, but we're learning that many of the residents are having difficulty dealing with the structure and rules that are necessary when you have people living in close prox-imity to one another. Many people are requesting – actu-ally they are demanding – to leave the cities."

"Why not just let them go? If they want to live like beg-gars, then let them."

"It's not that easy, Rick. I want those people in the trailer cities, not bothering those in the Employed and Wealthy classes. That means the challenge – your objective as Commandant – is to keep those people from leaving."

"Pardon me, Colonel. But if that's our objective, the trailer cities are no better than prison camps."

"There's more to it than that, Rick. The underclass has become a nuisance – a heavy weight that's dragging the rest of civilized society down. You know damn well that resources are limited – there's not enough oil or food or water for everyone. It's become necessary to reduce the population so that those remaining will be able to live comfortable lives."

"I'm afraid that I'm not following you."

"Rick...when I tell you the rest of my plan, then you are on my team. There's no turning back. Do you understand what I'm saying?"

"I guess so," Randall said tentatively.

"I have gained control over approximately two-thirds of the nuclear missiles in the country. The missiles are armed and can be launched at my command from the NORAD facility. I'm going to use some of those missiles to wipe out the underclass. Within four weeks, the relocation cities will be nothing but ashes and radioactive waste. And three-quarters of the lower class in my region will be history. We'll deal with the rest of them after that."

Rick Randall's face turned ghost-white. "Who in Washington came up with this plan?" he asked, already knowing what the answer would be. This plan could not have been approved by Washington. Nefario was going rogue, a possibility that Rick Randall suffered frequent nightmares about over the past six months.

"This isn't the government's plan. It's mine. Within two weeks, we're bombing a relocation city to send a message to the idiots in Washington that I hold the cards now. There will be no elections, no more Board of Directors making decisions for the country. I'll be running the show. If they refuse, I'll drop a nuke on every major city on the East Coast, starting with Washington D.C."

"I don't know what to say," Randall mumbled.

"Like I said, Rick, at this point you no longer have a choice. Or maybe you do have a choice. You can be a part of the plan and reap the tremendous rewards that await us, or you can be dead."

Rick Randall mumbled a weak agreement and then drove in silence for a long time. He never imagined that his military service would lead to this. He was so happy and proud when he thought Nefario was trying to lead the government to help the lower class build better lives. He still believed in his country, and now he had become an unwilling player in what amounted to a military coup. *I've got to figure out some way to stop this*, he thought.

Entry Forty-Two: November 2025

The Freedom Troopers had Patrick and his companion in their sights and were closing in fast, but fortunately they were still about fifty yards away. Patrick whispered to the other man, "Follow me around this corner. When we're out of sight, ditch your tool box under the steps of this trailer. We may still be able to get out of this, but if they find our tool boxes, we're dead."

After they stashed their tool boxes out of sight, the two rebels dashed down a gravel street. "Let's see if we can outrun these guys," Patrick said.

It looked like they had put some distance between them and the chasing Troopers, but then Patrick saw trouble ahead. Four Troopers were directly ahead with rifles aimed at the two rebels.

"Shit! There's no point in running. Put your hands up. And let me do the talking," Patrick said under his breath.

"All right, you two," one of the Freedom Troopers said. "What are you doing running around in the middle of the night? Let me see your ID cards."

"Don't have any," Patrick answered.

"Why are you dressed all in black?" the Trooper said as he searched them. At that moment, the Trooper found the black marker in Patrick's pocket. "So, are you the ones who've been writing on the posters all over the city?"

"I don't know what you're talking about. We're just out for a walk," Patrick said, trying to be as casual as possible.

"Bring them both into the station," the Trooper ordered his men.

***

Patrick and the other rebel were placed in separate rooms. As Patrick sat alone, he wondered if his companion would be able to hold out under interrogation. If he cracked, would he give up the entire group that had come to the trailer city? Would he tell them Patrick held some sort of leadership role in the rebellion? Would he tell them everything, including information about the dormitory?

This could be very, very bad, Patrick thought.

Months before, Jimmy and Patrick had discussed the possibility of having the rebels, especially those in command positions, carry a poison pill of some kind. If captured, they could opt for suicide instead of facing a painful and inevitable death by torture. Jimmy had actually decided to pursue the idea, but was never able to find a source for a reliable poison. Patrick found himself daydreaming about whether or not he would have taken the pill if he had one.

An hour passed, then two hours. Patrick could hear screaming in the distance, horrible screams of pain and terror. He worried about the other six men on his team. Would his companion give them up? Would Patrick give them up under the torture he was sure to suffer? He wondered what horrors the goons had in store for him.

Finally, the door opened and a Freedom Trooper walked in, holding a pair of handcuffs. "Stand up, you filthy infidel. It's your lucky day. Your friend says you're quite an important person. You're going to a holding cell until the Commandant arrives here tomorrow afternoon. When he found out we caught such a big fish, he said he wanted to interrogate you personally."

They walked down a long hallway of cells, and the Trooper pushed Patrick roughly into an open one and locked the door. "I'd get some sleep so you're wide awake for your interrogation tomorrow," the Trooper said with a vicious laugh.

***

The tortured rebel gave up Patrick as a leader of the rebellion, but protected the rest of the team. The others passed through the gate without incident and hopped into the waiting delivery truck. Kristina was waiting in the back compartment alone.

"Where is Patrick?" she asked quietly.

"He and his partner didn't come through the gate with us. They were nowhere to be seen."

Kristina pounded on the back of the truck cab and screamed, "Stop! Stop! We have to wait for him!"

One of the other team members touched Kristina's shoulder gently and said, "You know what our orders are. If they weren't at the gate at 07:00 hours we were to leave without them. We can't risk all of us being caught waiting for them. I'm sorry." The truck drove off.

***

Captain Rick Randall walked through the trailer city toward the prison facility. Everywhere he looked, government posters were defaced with rebel slogans:

GET OUT WHILE YOU CAN!

ESCAPE FROM THE CONCENTRATION CAMPS!

IS THIS REALLY A BETTER LIFE?

DEMAND THE FREEDOM TO CHOOSE

He walked into the building. Every Freedom Trooper stopped what they were doing and saluted him as he walked by. He stopped at the door of the Chief of Security's office. "Bring the prisoner into an interrogation room. I will question him personally."

"Of course, sir," the chief answered, "I'll be happy to assist you."

"Thank you for the offer, but it's not necessary. I'll interrogate him alone," Randall answered.

"That's quite unusual sir, if you don't mind my saying. Policy says that at least two government personnel be involved in all interrogation sessions."

"There's a new policy about that," the Commandant said sternly, "you'll get the memo in a day or two."

"Very well, sir. Go down this hallway to the third room on the left. We'll bring him in there. We'll leave his handcuffs on, of course. Do you need any instruments?"

"Not right now," Randall answered.

The Freedom Troopers shoved Patrick into the interrogation room. "That's all, I'll take it from here," Rick Randall said.

Patrick sat down and looked at the Commandant. He was expecting that huge, scary guy with all the medals that he ran into a couple of weeks earlier, and was relieved to see someone less menacing.

"So, you are the great Patrick, one of the leaders of the revolution," Randall said, and let the sentence hang in the air. Patrick answered with complete silence.

"Don't make this any more difficult than it needs to be. Look at me. I don't have any weapons. I'm not going to torture you. Let's just have a nice discussion."

Patrick raised his eyebrows and looked at Randall as if he had grown a second head.

"You're going to have to trust me," Randall said, "I'm being straight with you."

"Trust you? Are you crazy?" Patrick said, finally breaking his silence.

"I'll make you a deal. I want you to answer one question for me – just one question. Then I'll tell you why I asked it. But you must give me a straight and honest answer. Does that sound all right?"

"We'll see."

"How many rebel soldiers do you have under your command, and do you have transportation for them to Colorado?"

Patrick sat silent for a minute. It was not the question he was expecting. He weighed the impact of giving Randall that particular information and decided to take a chance. They probably already knew that he had hundreds of rebels at his disposal, so he wouldn't be telling them anything they didn't already know. "About six hundred rebels, all with the latest armament. I don't know for sure about transportation but we can probably get them all to Colorado."

Randall smiled and said, "Thank you. Now I'm going to share some information with you." He told Patrick about the missiles, NORAD, and Nefario's plan to wipe out the lower class and overthrow the government. "I can tell you this: whatever atrocities you think the government is committing now, they will be ten times worse under Nefario."

"I think I see what you're getting at," Patrick said, "but why the rebels? Shouldn't you report this to someone in Washington and let them handle it?"

"Colonel Nefario has a very strong network of contacts in Washington. I'm certain he still has people loyal to him in the Pentagon. I'm not sure who I can trust in Washington. If I tell the wrong person and Nefario found out I informed, I would suffer a horrible death."

"Are you sure this is a battle that the rebels can win? I don't want to send hundreds of men on a suicide mission."

"Nefario has two hundred Freedom Troopers at most guarding NORAD headquarters. He counts on the fact that it's built into the middle of a mountain to protect him. Plus there just aren't many troops available because so many of them are stationed at the relocation cities. I can get you past the main barricade into the mountain, which is the hard part, but you will have to take it from there. The important thing is that Nefario doesn't get a chance to launch those missiles."

"I'm not a college educated military officer like you," Patrick said sarcastically, "but I can see all sorts of logistical problems with your plan. What about satellite surveillance? Several hundred rebels traveling from the Midwest are sure to be noticed."

"As the Commandant of the relocation centers, I will request that the satellites focus on those for a few days to take the heat off you. I'll say that there have been too many escapes. For your part, you should not travel as one large group. And move mostly at night, stay under cover during the day."

"How will we communicate?" Patrick asked.

"I'll provide you with a two-way radio. I know there are a lot of details to work out. But we both want the same thing. Nefario plans to commit genocide and we have to prevent it. The future of the country is in our hands, you and me."

The two men talked for the next three hours, discussing contingencies and strategies. When they were finished, Patrick asked, "What happens to me now? I'm not going to do you any good sitting in jail."

Randall frowned and said, "That guy who was with you

and gave you up as a rebel leader? We're going to have to sacrifice him. If you do exactly as I say, you'll be out of here within the hour. Sit on the floor in the corner and look down at your feet. No matter what I say, don't look up," Randall said. He got up and threw the door open. "Chief! Get in here right now!"

The officer ran down the hall to the open room. "What is it, sir?"

"Who interrogated the other prisoner?"

"Two of my best Troopers questioned him. He confessed after two hours. These two were defacing posters with rebel propaganda slogans. This one," he said, pointing at Patrick, "is the leader of the local rebels."

"This one," Randall said angrily, "is a half-wit who your prisoner convinced to assist him. He has trouble spelling C-A-T, let alone writing any slogans. He was nothing more than a lookout for the man that you questioned. Neither one has an ID because they snuck into the city a week ago and have been squatting in an empty trailer. Why did you waste my time on this bullshit?"

"With all due respect, sir," the chief said shakily, "my Troopers are very capable at interrogation."

"Then they should know that when you torture someone, they'll tell you anything you want to hear, and it probably won't be the truth," Randall said sternly, "the proper way to interrogate someone is to first assess their mental state. If your men had taken the time to do that, they would have known they were questioning a pathological liar who had escaped from a treatment center and imagined himself a part of the rebellion. He recruited this poor moron to be his sidekick. When your men tortured him, he concocted the story about this man being a rebel leader to avoid further pain."

The man looked at the floor, "I see your point, sir."

"I don't want to waste any more time with these two. I'm leaving in a few minutes. I'll take this idiot with me and dump him in the nearest town so he doesn't bother you anymore. We will make an example of the other one. Execute him and then post photos. That should put an end to defacing posters."

"Shouldn't we interrogate him more thoroughly before we execute him?" the chief asked.

"That man is nothing more than a mentally ill squatter with delusions that he's part of the rebellion," Randall said. "Torture him and he'll just tell you more grand fantasies. Execute him immediately. In fact, bring him in here now."

A few minutes later, two Freedom Troopers dragged the other rebel into the small interrogation room. The man's face was covered in dry blood and his eyes were filled with a crazed terror. Randall stood up and faced the rebel.

"I want you to confess right now that your story was fabricated. Admit that both you and your dim-witted friend are just a pair of low-life vandals, not part of the rebellion."

The rebel was silent but Patrick could see him thinking through the possibilities. He knew that his only chance of staying alive was to play along.

"You're right! We just got drunk last night and decided to write on the signs! I'm sorry I lied!"

Rick Randall pulled his pistol and fired three quick shots into the rebel's face.

"Holy crap," one of the Freedom Troopers who had been watching mumbled to his companion. "Clean up in aisle three."

"Get a picture of the body, and put it on posters all over the city. Under the picture, say this is what happens to those who deface government property."

Patrick had new respect for the young Captain. He was smart enough to realize that if the other prisoner were kept alive and questioned further, eventually his interrogators would realize he was telling the truth about Patrick.

They drove about twenty miles toward Center City, and the Captain pulled the car to the side of the road. "I'm heading to the airport," he said to Patrick, "you or someone you trust needs to meet me at the time and place we agreed on. At that time, I'll give you the two-way radio and we'll make final plans. We've got a few weeks at most so this has to happen fast."

Entry Forty-Three: November 2025

"Are you sure about this Captain Randall?" Jimmy asked incredulously after Patrick finished telling him the story.

"Why else would he let me go without questioning me at all? The only information he has is that we have six hundred active rebels, and he probably already knew that. After he dropped me off, I made sure that no one followed me. They didn't have a chance to do any sort of GPS tracking implant, I was conscious the whole time."

"This makes me nervous," Jimmy said, "Mark, can you check out Rick Randall?"

"Be careful with that," Patrick pleaded, "he's the only way we're getting into that mountain. He described the NORAD facility; it has eight-inch thick steel doors. We can't afford to have suspicion cast on him."

"I'll be discrete," Mark Johnson said, "I know that Nefario has moved the Regional Command to Colorado Springs, so that much of his story is true."

"We don't have a lot of time," Patrick said, "so let's operate under the assumption we're doing it. Mark, do we have enough trucks for all of our people?"

"You won't be riding in grand style," Mark answered, "but we can do it."

"I don't mind being a little uncomfortable," Jimmy said.

"You said you've retired from military missions," Patrick said. "I think you should stay home for this one."

"No way!" Jimmy said loudly. "Listen, Patrick. If what you say is true, this is for all the marbles. I haven't got much time left. If something happens to me, I want to go out in style."

"I'm not sure about that," Patrick said uncertainly, "to be perfectly honest, what if you have a heart attack at the wrong moment, Jimmy? You could get us all killed."

"I'm not asking to be a leader; I'll just be one of the soldiers. If something happens to me, leave me behind," Jimmy said.

"All right, all right," Mark said, "you're in, Jimmy." Patrick shot a quick look at Johnson. What was he doing making operational decisions?

To break the tension, Jimmy changed the subject to the upcoming elections. "Mark, what are you hearing about the upcoming elections? Is there any chance they'll be fair?"

"Believe it or not, the people in Washington are opening

things up a little bit. There will be two people running for every major office. Both choices will be appointed to be on the ballot, there were no primaries or anything like that. But it's a step in the right direction."

"It'll be interesting to see how many people actually vote," Patrick said.

"That was the most disappointing thing about the elections in the old days," Jimmy said, "the number of people who voted was never very good. A little over half of eligible voters participated in Presidential elections and even fewer than that voted in mid-term elections where Congressional races were decided. It was like people didn't care."

"You're right, Jimmy," Mr. Johnson said, "and there may still be a problem with the turnout in the upcoming election. People need a government ID card to vote and many in the underclass don't have an ID. However, in Washington they're leaning toward allowing people living in the relocation cities to vote. If they do, that would really boost the turnout, at least in this region."

"Still, the candidates are hand-picked by the government," Patrick said.

"True, but like I said, it's a step forward. You guys should feel good about that – it was pressure from the rebels that forced the government to hold elections. Maybe they're just trying to give the illusion of democracy, but who knows where it will lead?" Mark said.

***

Three days after Patrick was arrested and released, Kristina met Rick Randall at the agreed-upon location. A dozen armed rebels followed her there and hid strategically where they could observe the building where the meeting took place.

"I'm Captain Randall," Rick said, extending his hand.

"You don't need to know my name. I suppose I should say thank you for releasing my boyfriend unharmed. But it's because of assholes like you that he was arrested in the first place."

Rick Randall stayed calm and said, "We're on the same side right now, so let's try to cooperate. Here's the two-way radio. It works on regular power or battery. You've also got an extra battery, just in case. I'm the only one who has a radio on the same frequency, and it uses the latest encoding scheme. Obviously, don't let this get into the wrong hands."

"Patrick said to tell you that we'll be ready to leave a week from today," Kristina said.

"And then add two more days for travel? Nine days from now is cutting it close. Nefario has an itchy trigger finger," Rick Randall said.

"This is a major operation and there's a ton of preparation," Kristina answered, "but I'll talk to Patrick and see if we can move it up. It won't be by more than a day or so."

"I have some good news for you. I've secured fifteen troop carrier vehicles. Each one holds about forty soldiers and their weaponry. They are top of the line vehicles. Military trucks should allow you to move relatively unnoticed. I'm still going to divert the satellite surveillance and I'll have a cover story in case somebody asks questions about troop movements in the area. I'll have the trucks ready for you in three days."

"Good. I'll tell Patrick to contact you every day at 6 a.m. He gets up early and you seem like an early riser.

Randall agreed and they ended their meeting.

Entry Forty-Four: November 2025

Of the rebels that snuck into the trailer cities, Patrick's group was the only one that encountered government soldiers. The combination of the slogans on government posters and the growing realization among residents that they were prisoners in the cities caused widespread demonstrations to break out.

In the relocation facility near Center City, one family was arguing bitterly about their living conditions. The husband had been a rebel in Patrick's squad, but his wife was one of many people who succumbed to the government's promise about a better life if they relocated and she insisted that they move into a trailer city.

"I hope you realize now, Darlene, what a stupid move this was," the husband said.

"Is life really so bad here, Ed? We've got food, shelter and you have a job – if you ever bothered showing up for it, instead of marching down the street demonstrating with your stupid buddies," Darlene snapped back.

"We're prisoners! This is no way to live. I'm fighting for our freedom, our basic rights."

"For a change, why don't you go fight for a paycheck? The kids need new boots for the winter."

"Fuck you, Darlene," Ed shouted as he stormed out the door. He went straight for the home of his friend, Franklin, and pounded on the door.

"Hey, Ed. What's up this morning?"

"I've fucking had it, that's what. I say today's the day that we get together and storm the gate. Make them let us out of here."

Ed and Franklin headed for the one and only tavern in the city. Even early in the day, the bar was crowded with other men who were skipping work. Most of them were familiar faces Ed had seen in demonstration marches.

Franklin could feel Ed's agitation and tried to calm him down. "Let's have a couple of beers and relax, buddy. Don't do anything crazy."

As they drank, Ed tried to relax but he couldn't. Something was very wrong with the relocation cities; he could sense it but couldn't put his finger on it. The people were like animals in a zoo – well fed and housed – but they were caged and trapped against their will.

Suddenly, Ed jumped up onto the bar. "Give me your attention! Listen to me! Are you tired of being stuck in this shit hole? Why can't we come and go as we please?"

"Shut up and let me drink in peace, you sound like my wife," one bar patron shouted back.

But another man yelled, "Let him speak! He's right! Have you seen them putting up cameras? And guard towers! This place is starting to look like a Nazi prison camp!"

"Why can't I leave the city for a day to visit my relatives?" another man shouted, "what are they afraid of?"

"Did you hear what happened to my husband the other night?" a woman said. "He heard his mother was very ill and tried to leave to visit her – they beat him up and he's still in the hospital!"

Ed shouted, "Let's storm the gate – right now! Show them who's really in charge!" He walked out the door, followed by at least fifty people. The crowd swelled to a hundred by the time they reached the gate area as people left their trailer houses to join the demonstration.

The mob approached the gate and was met by a small group of Freedom Troopers. One of the Troopers was on his radio, frantically calling for reinforcements. The Freedom Troopers blocked the gate and raised their rifles. It was a standoff.

Within a minute, Ed looked to his right and saw a column of twenty Troopers coming, all wearing gas masks. He turned to his left and saw the same thing, about twenty more Troopers approaching. It was now or never.

"Let's go!" Ed screamed as he ran for the gate. The mob followed him, shouting and pushing as hard as they could toward the wide gate.

The Freedom Troopers standing at the gate fired, but only managed to hit a small number of the rioters. The rest were now pushing at the gate fence and it was starting to give way. Gas clouds began filling the air as the other Troopers launched grenades into the crowd. The rioters who didn't succumb to the gas picked up scrap wood, anything they could find, and began beating the Freedom Troopers.

Every Freedom Trooper was now rushing toward the gate area as word of the riot spread throughout the city. Within fifteen minutes, there were over three hundred residents at the gate and an equal number of Freedom Troopers.

"They're pulling out red gas canisters!" one of the rioters screamed. Freedom Troopers had two levels of gas weapons. Blue gas grenades released a powerful tear gas and were typically used for crowd control. But stories had circulated among the lower class about the red gas canisters, which were being used more and more. The red gas was highly toxic and caused permanent nerve damage, sometimes even death.

The rioters tried to scatter, but were surrounded by Freedom Troopers who were beating them with their rifle butts and firing wildly into the crowd. Only two red gas canisters were needed to quiet the crowd, many of whom fell to the ground and lay motionless. The heavy metal fence gate still stood but was leaning precariously where the crowd had tried to push through it.

Ed's wife Darlene had heard about the disturbance and followed the crowd to the gate area, but hung back with other onlookers. After the disturbance ended, she carefully approached the bodies scattered on the ground, desperately hoping that Ed was not one of them. When she spotted Ed on the ground, she ran to him and knelt next to his motionless body, feeling for a pulse. There was none. Blood dripped slowly from a bullet hole under his eye.

***

Colonel Nefario slammed his desk and glared at Rick Randall. "You're supposed to be controlling the vermin in the relocation centers! Every single trailer city has experienced riots, and those that aren't rioting are figuring out ways escape. I've heard the reports so don't bullshit me. Troopers are taking bribes to let people out – money, sex, you name it. Others have taken advantage of the guards' inattention and cut through the fences. Thousands of people have escaped."

"We're understaffed. There are twenty thousand residents and only a few hundred guards per city. Rumors are rampant about residents being killed in riots. People are afraid."

"Where are these people going when they escape?"

"There are a couple thousand escapees from the reloca-tion cities making their way out of this region. They've heard that this is the only region with relocation cities."

"It's time to move forward then," Nefario said, "I'd like to have a few more days but we can't wait."

Entry Forty-Five: November 2025

"The satellite has detected something – something really big," the technician shouted to his supervisor. The supervisor took one look at what was unfolding on the surveillance monitor and called the Supreme Commander's office. As usual, he ended up talking to an assistant.

"This is Lieutenant Baxter in the satellite monitoring center. One of our satellites has detected a massive explosion in the Near West Region. The magnitude is significant enough to be a nuclear blast."

"Jesus Christ," the assistant said, "transmit a scan over here right now."

Meanwhile, one of the many data analysts in the satellite monitoring center was also looking at the screenshot. "Definitely a nuke," he said matter-of-factly, "looks like a smaller one. But it's nuclear explosion without a doubt."

The next call to the Supreme Commander's assistant was from Victor Nefario.

"Put him right through to me," the Supreme Commander growled. "Victor, what in blazes is going on out there? We've detected a nuclear explosion in your region."

"You are correct," Nefario answered casually, "I decided to nuke one of the relocation centers. It was just a small one so try not to get too worked up."

"You nuked a relocation center? What the fuck is wrong with you? You realize I'll have you busted and charged with murder for this!"

"Shut up and listen or the next one will land right on your fat head," Nefario said, "I have control over the nuclear missiles, not only in the Near West region but in most of the country. Get the Board of Directors together and tell them I want to talk with them. Do this within the next two hours or there will be another nuclear explosion."

Next, Nefario summoned Rick Randall to his office. "Richard, I have good news for you. You have one less relocation city to worry about."

Rick Randall was taken by surprise, "Why is that, sir?"

Nefario laughed and said, "You know Center Number Eight? The one located in what used to be the western part of Iowa? It's gone – I blew it off the face of the earth."

"Are you serious? That was one of the smallest and most remote of the trailer cities, but there were over five thousand people living there!"

"I know, isn't it great?" Nefario asked with a broad smile. "But enough celebrating. I need you to make sure that this news is contained. I don't want word of this spreading to the other relocation cities just yet. It would create a mass panic."

"You mean there would be mass escapes," Randall answered bitterly.

"Also, be sure to step up security. Send out a message to the relocation cities that there was a gas explosion at Center Number Eight, but that we have corrected the cause and the other cities have nothing to worry about. Got it?"

"Yes sir, will do," Randall answered.

"This bombing was a demonstration to those fools in Washington. If I don't have the keys to the kingdom within seventy-two hours, the nukes will start to fly. I'll start with the rest of the trailer cities. They're history one way or the other anyway. If they still don't see it my way I'll start bombing the East Coast."

Rick Randall recognized that his best chance to stop Nefario was to go along for the time being. The rebels reported that they were on their way, but they were still a day from Colorado Springs. Unfortunately, it was too late to request that the satellites be redirected to focus on the relocation cities. Hopefully the people in Washington had enough to worry about and wouldn't notice the movement of troop carriers toward Colorado. He decided to gather some information from the Colonel.

"I know it's not my concern sir, but with this recent development, did you increase the guards here in Cheyenne Mountain?"

"No, but don't worry about it," Nefario laughed, "We're in the most secure facility on the planet. I have a hundred or so men on watch outside and nearly a hundred inside. If anyone approaches, we just close the door and stay inside. This place has enough supplies for at least a year."

"You're right, sir. Once we close that door, no one can get in unless we open it for them, right?"

Entry Forty-Six: November 2025

Rick Randall contrived an excuse to leave NORAD head-quarters, claiming that his wife was ill at home. Hopefully he wouldn't end up being locked out of the mountain. He dug in his closet, pulled out the secure radio he hid there and called Patrick.

"Where are you right now?" Randall asked.

"We're closing in. I think we should be there within ten hours," Patrick said, "Let's plan on you opening the door at 12:00 hours tomorrow. That will give us enough time to get in position." Rick Randall had supplied Patrick with a detailed map of the NORAD facility and the surrounding area. They had agreed on the exact path for approaching the mountain and what to do once the rebels arrived.

"All right, I'll make it happen," Randall answered. He kissed his wife goodbye, hopefully not for the last time, he thought to himself, and drove back to NORAD head-quarters.

***

Victor Nefario put his feet up on his desk and picked up a call from none other than the Supreme Commander.

"I'm your point of contact from here on in," the Supreme Commander said, "but I am sitting with the Board of Directors and have you on the speaker."

"Fantastic!" Nefario said with fake enthusiasm. "Gentlemen! What a pleasure to talk with you today!"

"Cut the bullshit," the Chairman said brusquely, "and tell us, Victor, what is it that you want?"

"The Near West, West and the Southwest regions are seceding. That is effective as soon as possible, December first at the latest. What I want is for you to do all the paperwork to make it nice and legal."

"Have you completely lost your mind?" the Chairman screamed. "You're trying to take over half the country!"

"I'm not trying, I *am* taking over half the country," Nefario said deliberately. He was relishing this conversation. He had played it out in his mind for months.

"Jesus, Victor. You're crazy to do this. You'll never make it work. We're sending troops to seize control of every missile silo and disarm the nukes."

"I have my own loyal troops stationed at every silo in this half of the country," Nefario said, "I'm not being unreasonable. You can have the missiles in the East. I have more than enough nukes to blow you and your Board of Directors off the planet."

"All we have to do is cut off your satellite communication link," the Supreme Commander said, "and you'll be out of business."

"Really?" Nefario asked, "Why didn't I think of that? Oh wait, I did think of it! I've got control of a couple of the satellites. You guys really don't understand your systems very well. And I have some very smart people working for me."

There was a lengthy silence. Obviously the Board didn't anticipate the Colonel's level of preparation.

"I'm feeling very impatient," Nefario said. "You know what I want. I know that deciding whether to agree to dismantle your precious nation is a difficult decision for you. So I'll give you until 12:00 hours tomorrow. Of course, that's unless I hear that any of my missile silos are attacked or you try to screw up my communications. If you do, I start firing my missiles – there will be no warning and no hesitation."

Entry Forty-Seven: November 2025

It took four hours from the time of the Board's phone conversation with Victor Nefario to receive a full technical report.

"He wasn't bluffing," said the head of government communications. "Somehow he has commandeered two satellites. We're locked out of them."

"Same thing with the missiles," the Supreme Commander added, "we've analyzed satellite photos and sent a few reconnaissance teams to the missile silos. Nefario has his own troops at every one we looked at. We could overcome them – we have more men on the ground than he does – but..."

"If we try to seize the silos, he might launch his missiles," the Chairman said.

"Let me make this clear. There is no doubt that he would launch them," the Supreme Commander said. "Nefario is a psychopath. He'll turn the country into a nuclear wasteland without a second thought."

"What if we strike first and drop a bomb on Colorado Springs?" one of the Board of Directors asked.

"We would destroy an entire city, kill thousands of people, and the mountain would probably be undamaged," the Supreme Commander answered, "The NORAD facility can take almost a direct hit."

"Anything we can do to disable his communications before he can react?" another Director asked.

The communications expert replied, "There's a possibility, but we are analyzing whether what can be done quickly enough to ensure there is no time for him to respond before he's cut off."

"If it doesn't work and Nefario has time to launch the weapons, the result would be complete devastation," the Chairman said, "so be damn sure it's going to work."

"I have my best people working on it, but it'll be late tomorrow before we know that for certain," the communications head answered.

"How about ground troops?" one of the Directors asked.

"Satellite surveillance shows he only has a handful of troops guarding the entrance to the mountain," the Supreme Commander answered, "but NORAD is designed to be extremely secure. We would have to get some extremely heavy artillery up a narrow mountain road, past Nefario's guards and lined up perfectly right in front of that steel door, so that we have a close range, direct shot at the entrance. That's the only way to get in unless we knock and they open the door for us."

"The latest satellite analysis says there are several troop carriers converging on Colorado Springs, enough to carry over five hundred men," the Chairman said.

The Supreme Commander looked baffled by the information. "I know his troop counts, and Nefario doesn't have five hundred men to spare in his region. He has almost all his men tied up in those relocation cities right now."

The Chairman threw up his hands in exasperation, "Jesus Christ! You don't know whether they're his men or not? Are they our soldiers?"

"Possibly, but I can't say with certainty who those men report to," the Commander responded.

"Maybe you should find out," the Chairman said dryly.

***

Like all of the trailer cities, the one nearest Center City was in a state of upheaval. Word of the explosion quickly leaked out to all the relocation cities and residents were meeting at the city's tavern to discuss whether they were in any danger.

"I think we're safe. They said they've solved the problem," one man said.

"You're crazy!" another shouted. "My cousin told me we need to get the hell out of here."

"Why are they keeping us penned up in this place? Something ain't right," a woman yelled.

"What do you suggest we do? The last time we stood up to the Freedom Troopers twenty people got killed."

Suddenly the door to the bar burst open and ten Freedom Troopers ran in, smashing anyone in their path with their rifle butts. As the Troopers wrecked the bar and broke all the bottles, the head Freedom Trooper said, "This establishment is now closed. Everyone needs to leave here at once. Go to your homes and stay there."

The crowd murmured among themselves for a minute, weighing the odds of overcoming the soldiers. The Freedom Troopers stood in combat ready positions.

"All right, we're leaving," one of the residents finally said. The rest of the bar patrons slowly followed.

Two of the bar customers were the couple who Patrick had spoken with weeks earlier. "I hope you realize that we're trapped here now," the man said to his wife, "and this was what you wanted."

As they walked toward their trailer, they saw Freedom Troopers tacking up signs that said:

NO PUBLIC GATHERINGS
PERMITTED UNTIL FURTHER
NOTICE BY ORDER OF
YOUR GOVERNMENT

"I know," she said through her sobs, "but I thought we were doing the best thing for our future!"

"We can't take this lying down," the husband answered, "we've got to try something. Let's go door-to-door and tell people we're all making a run for it at a certain time. How about if we tell everyone to make a run for the gate tomorrow night?"

"Let's do it," the woman answered, and they began a long, sleepless night of avoiding Freedom Trooper patrols and knocking on doors.

***

Patrick and Kristina sat nervously in the back of the lead troop carrier vehicle, with Jimmy sitting across from them. "Review the plan one more time," Jimmy said.

"Randall gave us a map showing the terrain. There are only two routes to get all of the rebels to the entrance. We're likely to be spotted by Nefario, but I was told he doesn't have many men guarding the entrance."

Suddenly, an explosion sounded from the front of the truck and the vehicle lurched to a stop.

"What's going on?" Patrick yelled to the driver.

"The road just blew up in front of me!" the driver shouted.

Before Patrick could even answer, eight men dressed in camouflage burst into the back of the compartment, aiming weapons at the rebels. The leader looked around at the group of men and women dressed in civilian clothes.

"Who *are* you people?" one of the men asked.

The rebels had instinctively put their hands over their heads in surrender. Jimmy kept his hands up and answered calmly, "Let's stay cool here. I think we might be on the same side. Patrick, explain to these gentlemen who we are and what we're doing."

Patrick gave a quick summary of the situation, careful to leave out the critical fact that someone from the inside would be giving the rebels access to the interior of the mountain fortress.

"We were sent by the government – the real government – to identify who you are. Things are so fucked up in Washington right now they didn't know if you were ours or theirs. It turns out you're neither," the lead commando chuckled.

"Help us get around the pile of rubble you made in the road," Jimmy said, "and ride with us. We need all the help we can get."

"We'll come along. But I have to report this to Washington. Otherwise they'll send the drones out to stop you."

***

Patrick listened while the commando leader made his report. "What happens from here?" he asked the leader.

"You heard what I told them. They're concerned that when the enemy spots all your troops coming toward the entrance – and they probably will spot us – they'll start launching nukes. But frankly, the Supreme Command sees you as harmless because there is no way you're getting into that mountain and Nefario knows it. They think you guys might be helpful in creating a diversion, give him something else to think about. They hope you'll keep him busy for a while to buy them more time to figure out how to stop him."

It was time to break the big news. "Patrick left an important piece of information out," Jimmy said, "we have someone on the inside who is going to let us in."

"Really?" the commando asked. "Do you guys have a plan for once you get in there? Maybe we can work together."

Patrick smiled and pulled out the map of the NORAD facility.

Entry Forty-Eight: November 2025

"There's an alternate roadway leading to the mountain entrance that's only used for emergencies," Patrick said as he pointed at the map and talked to the commandos. "According to our inside source, there are a lot of Troopers posted on the main road, but the secondary road is lightly guarded. We'll use the secondary road for our approach. With any luck we'll bypass most of the guards."

"But once the Troopers on the secondary road start shooting, the others will come running," the head commando said. "We need to take out the guards on the secondary road quietly."

"Isn't that what you do best?" Patrick asked the commandos. "Maybe you can go ahead of us through the woods and surprise them before they are able to react."

"That's a great idea. What's the plan once we're inside?" the commando asked.

"As you can see on the map, there are a number of separate buildings inside the mountain, but very few of them are being used. Nefario is supposed to be in this one,"

Patrick pointed again to the map, "and that's where the command center for the missiles is located. Once we're in, the plan is simple – we storm the command center building. We should outnumber Nefario's guards by a huge margin."

"The thing is," the head of the commandos said, "we can't give Nefario time to launch the missiles. Once he's aware of us being inside, we've got to get to him fast."

"You're right," Patrick said, "but with the advantage we have in manpower, we should be able to break through to the command center within a few minutes. Several of us are carrying e-bombs that will disable the electronics in the control room – if we can get close enough to use them."

"It looks like this could work," the commando said. "With your permission, I'd like to let Washington know about your plan. I'm worried that they may do something stupid before we get a chance to attack. If they spook Nefario, it could ruin everything."

Patrick looked at Jimmy, who had been listening to the discussion. Jimmy nodded and said, "It's your decision Patrick, but I'd hate to have those clowns in Washington screw up our plan. Usually I'd say the less they know, the better. But they should be aware that we have a way into the mountain and a good battle plan once we get in."

"Yeah," Patrick added confidently, "and tell them they

should sit tight until this afternoon. By then we'll have wiped out the control center."

****

The Chairman of the Board slammed his fist on the table. "You've got to be kidding me," he shouted at the Director of Communications, "you allowed Nefario to seize two satellites right under our noses and now you're saying there's no way we can get them back?"

"He recruited some very talented people to join his cause," the Director said, "and they had full security clearance."

One of the other Directors spoke up, "How about disarming the missiles?"

"No chance," the Security Director said, "it took Nefario months to get those missiles armed and they're spread all over the country. We don't have nearly enough missile technicians to get to all of them in less than a day."

"Not to mention he has guards stationed at most of the silos. We could overcome the guards at a few locations, but if we attack the guards they'll let him know and he'll start firing missiles," another Director said.

"What about the Missile Defense System?" another Director asked. "The system we spent billions on that's designed to protect us from nuclear missile attack. Why aren't we using that?"

The Chairman said impatiently, "That was one of the first solutions we looked at. The damned thing is designed to stop missiles from crossing over our borders. It doesn't do any good for missiles launched from within the country."

"Shit. We're completely screwed then," the Director said.

"Don't give up yet. The rebels may get in and destroy the control center. We now have a group of government commandos working with them, and they have told me the operation stands at least some chance of success," the Chairman said.

The Security Director added, "I think we can help the rebels by cooperating with Nefario for now. Tell him we're giving into his demand and we're working on the agreement document, but we need a couple of extra hours past the deadline."

"Let's see a show of hands," the Chairman said to the Board, "Who votes in favor of this plan?" The decision was unanimous: the rebels were the last hope.

***

The trailer cities were in a state of chaos. Demonstrations and riots at all of the relocation cities continued throughout the night and into the next morning. Rick Randall ordered the Freedom Troopers to control the crowds with non-lethal methods and to avoid shooting or use of the lethal red gas whenever possible. When Nefario learned of this, he summoned Randall to his office in the middle of the night.

"Jesus Christ, Rick!" Nefario screamed. "One of the security people from a relocation city just called me. He says his hands are tied because you won't let him use lethal force. Those vermin are all going to be dead in about twenty-four hours anyway. What the hell are you thinking?"

Rick Randall was ready for this question. He suspected all along that Nefario had some of the security personnel in the trailer cities reporting to him directly. "I understand your concern, sir. However, I feel that we need to keep up the pretense of normal operations as long as possible. If we start killing the thousands of residents who are protesting, it will only encourage the others to try mass escapes. If that happens, you'll be bombing empty trailer cities."

"I supposed you're right," Nefario said thoughtfully, "and we only have a day more to wait. By the way, I got good news from Washington earlier this evening."

"What was that?"

"They've given into my demands. The agreement should be ready to sign by mid-afternoon tomorrow. It's going to be an official treaty, signed by all the powers-that-be in Washington, recognizing the new country that I control."

Rick Randall kept a straight face but frowned inwardly. He had prayed it wouldn't come down to this. The future of America really had come down to him and the rebels. They were all that was left.

Entry Forty-Nine: November 2025

The rebels gathered under cover of dense trees five miles from NORAD headquarters. Patrick used a small speaker to address the group of several hundred.

"Speed is the most important thing," he reminded the soldiers. "Move quickly and try not to get entangled in long fights. We have a tremendous advantage in numbers and we have equal or superior weapons. Everyone should have reviewed the plan and be crystal-clear where we're going once we're in there."

Jimmy spoke up, "Head for the command center and whoever gets there first destroys the equipment and kills Nefario. Remember, we cannot afford to fail."

"He's right," Patrick shouted into the microphone, "The future is in our hands. Let's move out!"

The troop carriers took the soldiers to within a mile of the entrance, and the rebels traveled the rest of the way on foot.

"Are you holding up all right, Jimmy?" Kristina asked as

they walked up the steep incline. They were near the front of the column of rebel soldiers moving in a long line up the narrow strip of concrete.

"This altitude is getting to me a little," Jimmy said as he labored for breath, "but I wouldn't miss this for anything."

About halfway up the secondary road, the rebels saw the bodies of Freedom Troopers scattered alongside the roadway. "Looks like the commandos were successful," Jimmy said.

Another twenty minutes later, the rebels emerged onto the main road and saw the entrance to their right, just fifty yards away.

"The other guards must be stationed on the main road further down the mountain," Patrick said. "I think we've snuck past them. The entrance should open any moment now."

At that moment two things happened: The main entrance doors began to open slowly, and the bulk of Nefario's perimeter guards appeared about a hundred yards to the left, coming up the main road toward the entrance. Fortunately, they had not yet noticed the rebels ahead of them.

"Mike!" Patrick radioed to his second-in-command who was bringing up the rear of the column. "The door is opening but we've got a lot of Freedom Troopers coming up the main road. They haven't spotted us yet but they will any minute. I'm taking my guys into the mountain, but I need you and your men hold off those Troopers and keep them from following us in."

"Got it," he answered, and as Patrick and the front half of the rebel column headed through the entrance, Mike's men poured onto the main road and charged downhill at the guards.

***

A piercing alarm sounded inside the command center. "Why is the main entrance open? Why are the outside security cameras not working?" Colonel Nefario screamed. He immediately suspected a government trick of some kind and phoned the officer in charge of security at the entrance. There was no answer because the officer was dead on the floor, the back of his head bashed in by Rick Randall. Captain Dan Harris was also dead, shot in the head by Rick Randall and stuffed under his own desk.

"Get your ass over there and see what the problem is!" Nefario screamed at one of his assistants. "Close that door now!"

Rick Randall slipped back to his own office, locked the door and crawled under his desk. His plan was to hide out there until the battle was done. He hoped that the majority of the rebels would get into the mountain before Nefario reacted and closed the entrance.

Nearly two hundred rebels entered the mountain before the huge entrance door reclosed. Mike and his men fought to hold off the outside Troopers as the door closed completely. Jimmy turned to Patrick and said, "We still have them outnumbered, but we're more shorthanded than I thought we'd be. And obviously Nefario knows something's up. We've got to move quickly."

Patrick led the rebels through the wide, rock-lined passage. They were still nearly a quarter-mile from the command center building. As the group neared their target, they saw a small group of Freedom Troopers blocking the entrance. "Here we go," Patrick said.

Nefario's Freedom Troopers were not only outnumbered, but the rebels also had heavy machine guns and small rocket launchers. Within two minutes, the Freedom Troopers were overcome and the rebels approached the command center building.

Patrick, Jimmy, Kristina and about twenty other rebels had just burst into the entrance when they heard an explosion behind them. One of the mortally wounded Freedom Troopers had set off a hand grenade as the bulk of the rebels passed. The shrapnel wiped out all of the rebels except for the small group who had already entered the command center. To make matters worse, there were several Freedom Troopers guarding the door to Nefario's inner sanctum.

The rebels scattered and quickly took cover behind various desks and pieces of equipment. The room was large, but with several rebels and Freedom Troopers packed into it, everyone was holding their fire for fear of hitting someone on their own side.

"If we can draw those Freedom Troopers away from that door," Jimmy whispered to Patrick, "a few of us can slip in and get to Nefario. We don't have much time to screw around."

Patrick pointed to two rebels who were hiding with Jimmy and whispered, "The rest of us will distract the Troopers and lead them out of here. As soon as it's clear, you three sneak into the command room."

Patrick stood up and yelled, "Rebels! Retreat now – out the door!" Gunfire and smoke filled the room as the rebels shot at the Troopers to cover their exit and the Troopers returned fire. In the meantime, Jimmy and the two men hid behind a large desk until the last of the Troopers left in pursuit of the retreating rebels. Then Jimmy planted an explosive charge on the heavy metal door leading to the control room.

Meanwhile, Nefario was desperately trying to figure out the workings of the missile control panel without success. "Where the fuck is Harris? Does anyone else know how to operate this thing?" he screamed.

The explosion blew the door off its hinges and the three men ran in. The moment the door was down, Jimmy rolled an e-bomb toward the missile control panel. The impact of the e-bomb was hardly felt by anyone in the room, but it created an ion storm than destroyed the electronics in the control panel and rendered it useless.

"Shit! You fucks will pay for that!" Nefario shouted as he and his three assistants started shooting. The rebels returned fire and Nefario's three guards fell to the floor.

Just when Jimmy thought they had won the battle, Nefario pulled out a machine gun that was hidden under the control console and started firing. Within seconds the two rebels who came into the room with Jimmy were mortally wounded and Jimmy felt a searing pain in his left arm where a bullet ripped through it.

Jimmy threw himself on the floor and took cover behind a large computer. He carefully peeked around and saw Nefario's leg sticking out from behind the main control console. From the angle of his foot, Jimmy was certain that Nefario had been wounded as well.

"Are you ready to surrender?" Jimmy asked with as much bluster as he could gather.

He heard Nefario wheeze, "Go fuck yourself," followed by a wet cough. The guy was definitely hit badly, Jimmy thought.

"Your control panel is fried. You won't be launching any nuclear bombs today. Looks like your time as a dictator was short lived," Jimmy said sarcastically.

"Not yet!" Jimmy heard Nefario growl. He looked up to see the giant of a man on his feet and charging toward him. Before Jimmy could react, Nefario was on top of him, knocking his rifle away and pummeling him with bare fists.

Nefario stopped and looked down at Jimmy with disgust. "You ignorant do-gooder. You're too naïve to understand that even if you kill me, you're only killing one man. What you'll never destroy is man's desire to dominate, to rule over other men with complete power. If you had killed me, someone else would have taken my place."

With just one arm working and Nefario pinning him down, Jimmy had to pick his spot. Generating as much force as he could, he plunged his right fist into the large bloody spot on the front of Nefario's uniform.

"Arrrgh," Nefario cried, and his reaction gave Jimmy just enough of an opening to slip out from under the huge man's bulk. Jimmy scurried to the other side of the room and hid behind a cabinet. His rifle was nowhere to be seen. For one reason or another, Nefario wasn't using his machine gun. It was probably either jammed or he was out of ammo.

"Listen to me," Nefario said quietly, his wheeze now even more pronounced. "It seems to me that we have a stand-off. Maybe we can reach some sort of agreement. I don't think you understand the plans I have for the country. It really won't be that bad. How about if I give you an important role in the new government? You know, a job where you can do some good. I need a guy like you, a man of the people."

Jimmy was getting light-headed and weak. Blood was beginning to pool on the floor at his left side and there was a pain in his chest like he felt the night of the drone attack, only much, much worse. It was now or never.

"Sorry, but I respectfully decline your offer," Jimmy said as he stood up and walked toward Nefario. Victor Nefario stood up and faced Jimmy defiantly, his fists clenched.

"You want to fight me hand-to-hand? I'm betting on me," Nefario said smugly.

"You said man's lust for power will never die," Jimmy said, "you might be right, but there's something else that will always be true, and that's the desire for freedom. I may die today, but man's willingness to fight for freedom and justice will live forever. As for you and me, I'll see you in hell, you fucking asshole."

Jimmy was now just a few feet from Nefario. He grabbed a hand grenade from beneath his vest and pulled the pin. The last sight that Colonel Victor Nefario saw was Jimmy's grinning face.

Meanwhile, Patrick's group of rebels who retreated from

the control center building successfully held off the Freedom Troopers. The last of the Troopers had just fallen
dead when Patrick heard a loud explosion come from the
direction of the control room. He motioned for the rebels
to follow him into the building.

They walked carefully through the outer room and into
the rubble that was formerly the control room. It was
then that Patrick saw the bodies – Nefario and his three
guards, the two rebels and Jimmy.

"Oh, Christ," Patrick mumbled as he knelt next to Jimmy.
There was no doubt he was dead. Kristina quickly joined
Patrick at Jimmy's side and began weeping.

"This was the way he wanted to go," Patrick said quietly.
"He knew he didn't have long to live. I should have figured all along this was what he was going to do."

Patrick told the rebels to search for Rick Randall, reminding them that when they found him not to harm him. The
Captain was still hidden under his desk, the only government survivor of the attack on NORAD headquarters.

"Hey Randall!" Patrick called out when they finally found
him. "We did it! Nefario is dead."

"That's great!" Rick Randall answered. "I'm going to contact all of the relocation cities and order them to open the
gates and let the residents come and go as they want. But
first I'll open the door so you can get out of here."

Entry Fifty: November 2025

Rick Randall opened the main entrance and the rebels who had been waiting outside flooded into the side of the mountain.

"How did your guys do?" Patrick asked Mike.

"We lost a few men, but we won the battle. We wiped them out," Mike answered. "Is Nefario dead?"

"Yes," Kristina said solemnly, "and so is Jimmy." She told Mike the scene that they had found in the control room.

"We need to get all of the rebel bodies out of here," Patrick said, "I want them to be put to rest like the heroes that they are." The surviving rebels spent the next two hours focused on the sad task of loading bodies into one of the troop carriers.

Instead of a joyous celebration, the long trip back to Center City was quiet and subdued. Much of the discussion centered on what would happen to the government now that Nefario had been defeated. Patrick had brief communication with Mr. Johnson, who had requested that Patrick travel to Washington to meet as soon as he was able.

Patrick spent three days at home recovering from the battle and the trip back from Colorado. On the fourth day Kristina said to him, "Are you ready for your trip to Washington?"

"Only if you come with me," Patrick answered, "I just spoke with Mark Johnson and there will be a charter jet to pick us up at the airport in three hours. So pack a suitcase."

A large limousine was waiting on the runway as Patrick and Kristina deplaned in Washington. "Wow, I feel so important," Patrick mumbled to Kristina, "I wonder what this is all about."

Mr. Johnson was in the back of the limo and greeted Patrick and Kristina with a broad smile. "Welcome to Washington," he said. "I think you'll find things have changed quite a bit here in the past week."

"What do you mean?" Patrick asked.

"You have to understand, Patrick, that the government was never united. The faction that took control several years ago was made up of some pretty bad people. There were a number of others like me that didn't approve of what was going on. But we had to bide our time and work in the background."

"So that's why you and your friends supported the rebellion," Kristina said.

"That's right. Nefario's takeover caused a huge shakeup – after you guys took care of that lunatic, the Chairman resigned and so did most of the Board of Directors. The new Chairman is a supporter of mine, and he appointed me and several others with similar political views to the Board."

"Pardon me for not getting excited," Patrick said, "but so what? There's a new Board of Directors. How does that help the country?"

"It's a beginning," Mark answered. "We have already set a nationwide election for the first Tuesday in February. In June, there will be a Constitutional Convention that will be attended by elected representatives from all over the country. The goal will be to use the United States Constitution as a basis to create a modern Constitution. So that process doesn't drag on, we have mandated that the new Constitution be ratified on July 4, 2026."

"Exactly two-hundred-fifty years after the Declaration of Independence was adopted. Nice touch," Kristina said.

"I've grown pretty cynical over the past couple of years," Patrick said, "What's to stop the rich and powerful from taking over the whole process? Then we'll be right back where we started from."

"Me and my friends on the Board will do everything we can to prevent that," Mark Johnson said. "But you have to realize, things were never perfect in the United States. And they never will be perfect in the future, no matter what we try to do. There will always be some injustice and inequality, that's a part of life. The thing we must strive for is to keep those injustices and inequalities minor and not let them get out of control like they did in the past twenty-five years."

"You have good intentions, I can tell," Kristina said. "But why are Patrick and I here in Washington?"

"Patrick is going to address the new Board of Directors, and we also would like to make you the first nominee to be a delegate to the Constitutional Convention," Mark answered. "You're quite a hero here in Washington; some people are calling you the man who saved the nation."

"You're blushing, Patrick," Kristina laughed.

They continued to discuss the future as the car drove toward a beautiful Washington sunset. Patrick couldn't help but think that the worst was finally over. For the first time in his life, he was confident that America was headed toward a still uncertain, but definitely brighter, future.